VIRAGO
MODERN CLASSIC
401

Mae West

Mae West was born in 1893 to indulgent parents in Brooklyn. On the stage by the age of five and bent on a theatrical career by seven, she went into vaudeville at fifteen, often writing her own comic material. Her daring play, *Sex*, was a Broadway smash hit in 1926, but earned her a brief term of imprisonment for obscenity. She continued to write lively plays which were unusually frank for the era and in which she established her increasingly iconic persona – wisecracking, good-humoured and sexually predatory. Her play, *Diamond Lil*, opened in 1927 and was later filmed as *She Done Him Wrong*, which in its turn became a novel. A contract _____ her to Hollywood, where she kept _____ *Night* _____ *Goin'*

SHE DONE HIM WRONG

Mae West

Introduction by Kathy Lette

Published by VIRAGO PRESS Limited 1995
20 Vauxhall Bridge Road, London SW1V 2SA

Copyright © 1932 The Estate of Mae West

Introduction Copyright © Kathy Lette 1995

The right of Mae West to be identified as the author of this work has been
asserted in accordance with the Copyright, Designs and Patents Act, 1988

All rights reserved

A CIP catalogue record for this book is available from the British Library

Typeset by Keystroke, Jacaranda Lodge, Wolverhampton
Printed and bound in Great Britain by
Cox & Wyman Ltd, Reading, Berkshire

Introduction

'Is that a gun in your pocket, or are you just pleased to see me?'

'A hard man is good to find.'

'Goodness, what beautiful diamonds.' . . . 'Goodness had nothing to do with it, dearie.'

'Climbing the career ladder, wrong by wrong.'

'It's better to be looked over than overlooked.'

'Between two evils, I always pick the one I never tried before.'

'When I'm good, I'm very, very good, but when I'm bad I'm better.'

Lines like this have had audiences reeling from quip-lash for much of the twentieth century. Mae West had a black belt in the art of tongue-fu.

And then there's the body. Famous for breasts which arrived five minutes before *she* did, the Battle of Britain pilots named their inflatable chest life preservers 'Mae Wests'. From the makeshift airstrips in Egyptian deserts and Pacific islands, airmen flew into battle with her legs splay-painted on their fuselages, whilst beneath the waves those same legs trembled on the tattooed musculature of sailors manning allied submarines. And her lips – Salvador Dali designed a sofa of red silk made from enlarged photographs of Mae's mouth.

But apart from The Body, which makes every other female feel like a bag full of cold porridge, and The Wit, which should have been registered at Police Headquarters as a lethal weapon, what do we *really* know about her?

Mae West was born in 1893, the progeny of an unlikely coupling of a society beauty and a streetfighter nicknamed Battlin' Jack. By the time she died in 1980, her minestrone mix of talent had made her a successful comedienne, singer, dancer, playwright, director, actress, scriptwriter, producer, Sex Goddess and novelist. If this isn't enough to make any writer impale herself on her pen, Mae was also a feminist who makes Madonna look like Julie Andrews, an intellectual who rubbed shoulder pads with the Roosevelts (this woman plucked her highbrows) and a civil libertarian who went to jail in defence of freedom of expression.

To cap it all, she was a brilliant business woman, who insisted on creative control: she refused to sign any Hollywood contract unless it contained a clause that the completed film must in every way be 'to her satisfaction'. Today, when the only creative muscle exercised by cinema stars is in their control-top pantyhose and screen-writers are the most put-upon of literary prostitutes, we can only marvel at a woman who invented the 'droit morale' in her contracts with Paramount for the films she wrote (including *Night After Night, I'm No Angel, Belle of the Nineties* and *Goin' to Town*).

To me, what makes Mae West so fas-cin-at-in', apart from the fact that she left school at twelve (having left school myself at fifteen – the only examination I've ever passed is my pap test – I like nothing more than discovering autodidacts) is that she accomplished all this in an era when women were meant to be no more than decorative and domestic. West may have been decorative but her domesticity was limited to the sewing of wild oats and barbecuing of sacred cows – entire *herds*. All this makes Mae West worthy of re-discovery. Suddenly, her feminism seems no longer precocious, but a precursor of how it should be, in an age where women demand to be treated as equals instead of sequels.

Mae made her stage debut at five, eluding the watch-dogs of the Gerry Society, a child protection agency whose unexpected theatre visits would send little Buster Keaton scuttling into the nearest trunk. It was the time of 'Mr Bojangles', when a pre-tramp Charlie Chaplin was playing society drunks in imported London music hall acts, Groucho Marx was so young he was painting on his moustache and W.C. Fields (later her co-star in *My Little Chickadee*) had not yet contracted bottle-fatigue. These were her competitors, as she battled to keep out of the chorus and to rise to the top of the vaudeville bill.

It was also a time when women did not have the vote and mathematics was the main method of birth control. (Females who miscalculated in this ovarian roulette were called 'Mum'.) Margaret Sanger, an American midwife forbidden from studying to become a doctor, had to go to Holland to gather contraceptive information which she then published in pamphlet form in 1912. They were banned under Post Office legislation designed to prevent obscene material being sent through the post. In most American states, women were not allowed to testify in court, hold title to property, establish businesses, take out bank loans or sign papers as witnesses. Wedlock was little more than a padlock, with wives compelled to pledge obedience. 'Insanity' and 'moral unfitness' were grounds for men to divorce their wives, depriving them of their children and casting them forth from marriage bed to Bedlam. Most females faced an anorexic range of occupations: badly paid domestic or factory work for the poor and badly paid teaching or nursing for the better educated. Denied equal pay or equal access to education and the professions (Harvard Law School only admitted women in the 1950s); a woman's economic dependence on her man in the early twentieth century kept her tethered to the tea towel.

When it came to morality, the majority of men were Olympic Gold Medal Champions in Double Standards. Hypocrisy in sexual relations was endemic, in literature as much as in life. Pre-marital sex labelled a man as a 'man' ... and a female as a 'fallen woman', (in most cases, of course, she didn't fall, but was pushed). In books, sex was done in brackets. Foreplay, which consisted of lighting someone else's cigarette, was followed by an interval of asterisks. Women didn't have orgasms, they had a row of dots ...

Mae West fought the hypocrisy of the times with the only weapon available to her: shooting from the lip. West maintains that she became a writer by the accident of 'needing material and having no place to get it'. When producers found this material too controversial, she produced the plays herself. Her first play, which she wrote, directed and starred in, was coolly and simply called *Sex*. It was a smash hit on Broadway in 1926, even though New York newspapers were too prudish to accept advertisements for it. In it's forty-first sell-out week at Daly's theatre, it was raided by police, who sympathetically offered not to prosecute if she closed the play down. Mae chose to stand trial, courageously, as no court in the America of this prohibition era could be seen to tolerate immorality. The District Attorney had to concede that there was nothing lewd or lascivious in her script and that it was 'Miss West's personality, looks, walk, mannerisms and gestures which make the lines and situations suggestive' – especially her famous dance, the 'shimmy'. Just as Lenny Bruce, forty years later, was to claim that the obscenity was not in his act, but in the act of police officers who performed it in the witness box, so Mae West objected to being tried by hearsay.

She insisted on performing her 'shimmy' in the well of the court.

But obscenity is in the groin of the beholder. Mae's judge convicted her for 'corrupting the morals of youth', fined her $500 and sentenced her to a short spell on Devil's Island. She complained about her rough prison underwear and saw enough of homosexuality to write her next play about it, *The Drag*. The theatre management became nervous and asked for re-writes. Rather than dip her pen in disinfectant, West withdrew the play. But she was enough of a drawcard for the Biltmore Theatre to stage her next play, *The Pleasure Man* in 1928. Opening night saw an unscheduled third act; a team of New York's finest, brandishing their nightsticks, rushed on stage and arrested the entire cast. 'Mae West in Paddy wagon again' blared the headlines at the time, 'Bad Girl of Broadway in Trouble Once More'.

The instigator of this trouble was a fun-loving body called 'The Society for the Suppression of Vice', part of the 'moral purity' movement which was enormously powerful in America in the 20s. When it came to moral victories, these people were warmongers. The champagne-saturated, charlstoning image of America just before the Great Depression is historically false: the times were pious beyond belief. Mainstream America belonged to the bible-basher, campaigning against whisky and prostitution and demanding a rigid code of sexual behaviour from men and women alike. Many of these thin-lipped sexual McCarthyites were women who actually thought of themselves as 'feminists'. Ostensibly, the object of their concern was the young single woman who was now able to find work as a secretary or typist in cities on the East coast. A wholesome caricature of the new independent woman soon appeared: The Gibson Girl. She was dressed in a mannish blouse with a little tie at the high neck, a long dark skirt, glasses and 'follow me home and play scrabble' shoes. Always depicted as intensely serious, this woman couldn't crack a smile at a joke festival.

Mae West was her antithesis, and ultimately her antidote.

Through the seismic days of the Wall Street Crash, the gruelling Great Depression and the struggling New Deal, Mae West first mounted and stayed on her unique pedestal: an icon who raised eyebrows for a living. The box office declared her 'not guilty' on the grounds that the US Supreme Court was later to recognise as a defence to obscenity – she had a 'redeeming social purpose'. She combined sexuality with satire, at a time when America desperately needed a cure for its irony-deficiency.

'I could say almost anything, do almost anything on a stage,' West reveals in her autobiography, 'if I smiled and was properly ironic in delivering my dialogue.'

It was this irresistible mix of sexuality and self-mockery, which allowed Mae West to indulge her amorous philanthropy – 'Men are my kind of people, a favourite hobby' – and yet escape the social stigma of having what would be called these days 'margarine legs' – easily spread. Her dialogue was, moreover, a breath of fresh, one-liner-ed air beside the formalised heroines of the silent screen and the romantic tosh that crackled from soundtracks when they started to talk; a kind of verbal musak. As F. Scott Fitzgerald put it, 'In a world of Garbos, Barrymores, Harlowes, Valentinos and Clara Bows, Mae West is the only type with an ironic edge, a comic spark, that takes on a more cosmopolitan case of life's enjoyments.'

Reading between the lines of her autobiography, Mae's idea of fidelity was to only have one man in bed at a time, 'Getting down to your last man must be as bad as getting down to your last dollar.' Her obsession seemed to border on sexual kleptomania, 'Sometimes it seems to me I've known so many men that the FBI ought to come to me first to compare fingerprints.'

Perhaps she was just living down to her reputation. But in a letter to Dr Kinsey, of Kinsey Report fame, she struck an authentic note, 'Because I portray sex with humour and good nature instead of something shameful, I think my portrayals are accepted in the spirit in which I play them. I have excited and stimulated, but I have never demoralised.'

What a world away from the pornobabes of today, who wink and blush and masturbate into the vaselined lenses of 'glamour' photographers, or who bake their airbrushed brains on the beaches of *Baywatch*. During the Gulf War, the US Air Force showed hard-core movies to stoke its A-10 pilots up before they took off to blast the Iraqis (and occasionally their allies). I prefer to think of the men in their Spitfires and Kittyhawks and Hurricanes, Mae Wests around their shoulders, her skirt blown up behind their propellers. Mae West not only rescued sex from the prudery of The Gibson Girls, she positively gave it a good name.

When it came to work, West contracted a healthy dose of *sceptic*-aemia where Hollywood was concerned, 'I always held it at arm's length like a would-be-lover one didn't fully trust.' About her plays she said that they were 'soon finished, remembered only by photographs and yellowing reviews.' Whereas 'a book lasts as long as someone keeps it on a shelf.' What makes Mae West a good novelist, besides the verbal callisthenics and triple entendres, is the rhythm of her prose, her vivid characterisation and sharp ear for dialogue. As she said of herself, 'I ain't 'fraid of pushin' grammar around so long as it sounds good.'

Of course, what Mae West mostly wrote during her extraordinary life, were cheques. For diamonds. It was this passion for rock-solid investments which inspired her most famous creation, Diamond Lil.

She Done Him Wrong began life as a play, staged, as one critic put it 'by the grace of God and the laxity of the Police Department'. Mae West adapted and starred in the screen version before completing the novelisation in 1932. Sixty years later, the protagonist, Diamond Lil, has not yet passed her amuse-by-date. Despite the attempts of the God Squad to make a clean sweep of her dirty mind, this is a woman who gives good Hedonism. In Diamond Lil, men with money to burn, meet their match . . .

It has been a real pleasure to dive between these covers and discover the real Mae West: not just the unthinking man's Dorothy Parker, and certainly not the prototype for Marilyn Monroe (Mae would never have sung 'Mr President' with such simpering slaveishness).

The only drawback to spending time in Mae West's company is the danger of contracting one-liner-itis. I've been sashaying round with my hand on one hip, (not a good look with a baby on the other) rehearsing spontaneous husky-voiced quips for weeks now.

Yet despite her status as a cultural 'come up and see me sometime' icon, she remained down to earth; a self made woman, who didn't worship her creator. Mae West wrote her novels to disprove the accepted notion that, as a woman, it was considered stupid to be too clever. In a man's world, she had what it took to take what they had.

Kathy Lette, London 1995

1

◆◇◆

A PRISON CELL AND A BOUDOIR

'S O SHE went and done me dirt!'
Chick Clark muttered that refrain over and over
while his thick fingers clutched the iron bars of his cell
door. The 'grapevine' had brought him the news that his
woman had 'flew the coop'.

He looked up at the roof above the corridor and then
laughed shortly. 'I ain't so smart after all,' he told himself.
'I might've known that ice was hot. Givin' most of them
sparklers to Lil, and now rottin' in the pen for it. Ten years!
It's a hell of a long time. I wouldn't give a good goddam her
pullin' her freight on me, but she said she'd wait. She swore
like hell she'd stick. Jeez, her kisses was sweetest when she
lied to me!'

'Whatsa matter, cull?' came a voice from the next cell.
'You goin' soft in there talkin' to yerself like dat?'

'What's it to yer?' snarled Chick Clark.

'Aw, don't git yer hump up,' the voice replied. 'We all got
wind of yer trouble, cull. Take it easy, pal.'

Chick's hands tightened on the bars. For an instant
between those straining fingers he imagined the soft throat
of Diamond Lil. He closed them murderously. A sob tore
itself from his dry throat. Immediately after, he coughed
loudly so that the others wouldn't know that emotion had
got him for a moment.

Chick was good-looking in a rough-and-ready way. His eyes were dark and piercing and set too close together. Laugh wrinkles at the corners of them told that he could enjoy a joke. But his jaw was like a steel trap and his mouth was as cruel as a knife-cut.

Chicago Chick Clark, super-crook, fearless, sharp of mind, notorious as a master at jewel robbery, had let himself be ditched by a woman. That dose was more bitter than gall. The worst of it all was, he loved her. Yes, he loved Lil so goddam much he'd die for her. But he'd wring her neck and send her soul to hell before he'd see her in the arms of another man.

Ten years in Joliet was no picnic. You could stand it all right if your woman was waiting for you with soft arms and breasts when you came out. You could stand it if she wrote letters to you and told you you were still her man, even though she was lying like hell and was in bed with some other man before the ink hardly dried on the paper. You could even stand the gaff if she had to peddle her stuff on the streets while you did time. But to swear you'll stick and then take the breeze loaded down with the front you got sent up for givin' her. God, can a guy take that on the beak and like it? Not Chick Clark.

He spat viciously through the bars into the corridor. Then he wiped his hands on his prison trousers and went to sit on his bunk.

He began to think of their life together, Lil's and his. He had first seen her in a joint on State Street. He had been flush at the time, having just got rid of some hot stuff. She had looked so beautiful that she just took his breath away. There was nothing tough about her; she was young, her waist was like the stem of a wine-glass and her breasts were full and firm. Her eyes were large cool blue ponds, her hair was yellow as maize and she wore it in an astonishingly lovely style of her own. No, he had decided after staring at her for a long time, she was nothing like any of those scratchy-looking dames around there.

He had introduced himself, and having flashed his roll, he soon had Lil clinging to his arm while they strolled down State Street to the Palmer House bar. Later he had hired a smart-looking rig with a high-stepping horse, and they drove out along the lake front. It wasn't long before they were living together. When he cracked a crib and came off with a good haul of jewels he always kept out the diamonds for Lil. She loved diamonds. And he loved her.

A few brief years of happiness together and then the hand of the Law that had waited patiently so long reached out and flung him down in a prison cell for ten long years. As he sat on the edge of his bunk he groaned. Not because he was in the 'pen'. But Lil, who mattered most to him in the world, had streaked to New York as soon as the gates had clanged to behind him.

'Lil,' he murmured, rocking from side to side, 'why did yer do this to me? Whyn't yer keep yer word and wait? I'll get out. I'll get out of this blasted hole Lil! Lil! You know I'd croak fer yer. How could yer lay by me night after night and tell me things, and 'en soon as I get a bum steer quit me like a dirty rat?'

He sprang up and beat his fists against the walls of his cell till skin and blood from his knuckles streaked the plaster.

'Lil! Lil!' he shouted. 'Yer can't do it to me! Yer can't double-cross me and get away with it. I'll find yer, do yer hear? I'll get yer, damn your black soul to hell! I'll get yer!'

There were the sounds of running feet as two guards hustled towards Chick Clark's cell to silence him as only they know how to silence a prisoner.

Diamond Lil yawned prettily and stretched her pink, enamel-tipped toes. If she were a cat she would have purred, so contented was she at the moment. But Lil was never

3

contented for long. She let fall the pink-covered *Police Gazette*, having drained it of all juicy information. She was nestling luxuriously in a feather bed set very neatly in a huge gold swan, which appeared to be laying an egg on the floor of the boudoir. It never laid the egg, but it always looked very much as though it would enjoy it.

The swan bed had come from France, and Lil liked to consider the possible accomplishments of all the fair lights of love who had undulated their bodies in becoming emotions in perhaps the very spot on which she now reclined.

She liked, too, to lie there and survey the grandeur of this room which Gus Jordan had outfitted according to her smallest desire. Despite the fact that it was up over the saloon in Chatham Square, and that a stale smell of beer and whisky sours belched into the room whenever she opened the door, she liked the room. If she had had any regrets or felt any twinge of remorse over leaving Chick Clark to his fate, they were all dissipated by now.

Gus Jordan, the Boss of the Bowery, had seen to that. He had seen her in much the same manner as Chick. But this time she was dripping with the diamonds Chick had poured over her, and she was sitting in a stall at the Haymarket. She had been entertaining for the evening, a young man who was slightly drunk when she met him, and who was about to slide to the floor when Gus saw her. She saw Gus, too, and after a few discreet inquiries as to who the impressive bearded gentleman was, she let her companion complete his slide and joined, nicely invited, of course, Mr. Gus Jordan and his party.

Almost overnight, New York was conscious of Diamond Lil. Jordan saw to that. He was a power in ward politics. He was a ward-heeler of no mean talents, and he knew how to keep in the good graces of the Big Boys uptown in Fourteenth Street. His dance hall and bar-room had acquired a name far and wide, the well-earned and pleasant cognomen of 'Suicide Hall'. While no one had ever been discovered there in the state of *rigor mortis*, yet there was sufficient truth in the saying that the only dead ones at Gus's emporium were those his henchmen took down for a final helpless swim in the East River.

Gus was particularly proud that he could gather to himself one so exquisitely beautiful as Lil, because he was getting on in years. The fact that he could hold a woman like Lil was a tribute to his virility. So he thought.

He was a hard-fisted, hard-boiled manager of men. Shrewd, crafty, cold and deadly as steel in the conduct of business, he became red-hot molten metal when it came to Diamond Lil. He plastered her with diamonds, and when she raved over every new acquisition he was foolishly happy. She herself was like a beautiful stone – filled with languid, ambient fire and sparkle. And Gus believed that Lil loved him. But so did Chick Clark – once. Vanity of vanities! Could Diamond Lil love anyone more than herself? Love anything better than the white flame of her diamonds or the varied red flames of men's passions?

To put it frankly, Diamond Lil was a beautiful short course to Hell. She was a Charybdis in a modern setting of white ice. A feeder on men's souls with diamonds for dessert.

It was nice to lie in a gold swan bed: it was nicer still to have somebody give you diamonds. Men would wither and custom stale them, but diamonds! Ah, they were crystallized immortality! She felt that life would never go out of her while she covered her body with diamonds. How they glistened on her alabaster skin! No queen had been more lovely, she thought.

Lying there in the comfortable billows of the bed, Lil considered all these achievements of hers so far and she was more than satisfied with them. Suddenly she raised her voluptuous body that revealed every curve and dimple through the diaphanous nightdress, and swung her feet over the side and let them dangle for an instant. Then she drew on a robe and, thrusting her feet into dainty slippers, crossed to her dressing-table where her diamonds lay heaped from the night before. Bracelets, rings, pendants, necklaces, dog-collars, she let them ripple through her fingers with a feeling of exultation. They represented progress and conquest.

After a moment of fondling her treasures she turned from them and began to draw on black stockings; silk they were and from Paris, too. As she drew them up her shapely legs a knock came at her door. She let up the shade of the window and turned off the gas-jets. If it was Gus, as she expected it was, he would fuss if he found the gas lit at that hour. He was funny that way. He would buy her loads of diamonds, and yet complain about his gas bills.

She opened the door. The familiar smell of the bar-room below wafted up to her. Somebody, probably Ragtime Kelly, was pounding the piano down there and hitting the keys that just never were on the instrument. Gus loomed in front of her. His big bulk moved into the room. His hands were in his pockets, and he looked at her with a calm, self-satisfying relish. He presented a domineering, swaggering air, empha-sized by a surliness he practised under the mistaken idea that it became his importance as a political mogul.

Lil regarded him shrewdly for a moment. Jordan had moods. Some of them she ignored or crossed, according to her own whim at the moment. Of others, she tried to be one step ahead. She knew when to tell him to go to hell and when to allow him to coax her into his arms. This morning she decided that, whatever his temper, it didn't matter. She made a move to get into her dress.

'I'm in a hurry, Gus,' she said, although she had acted before his appearance as though she had had all the time in the world to waste. 'You know my pictures are supposed to be ready this morning. The photographer said he'd have them done. I want to get 'em and see how I look.'

'You know how you look,' Gus declared with an attempt at facetiousness which never became him. 'If you don't you can ask me. I'll tell you any time.'

He swung over to her dressing-table and his eyes under their shaggy brows reviewed the pieces of jewellery lying there. Suddenly his clumsy fingers dashed at a piece of icy fire and held it up.

'I ain't never seen this pendant before, have I?' he asked. 'Here's the mate to it. No, they ain't none of my gifts.'

'Well, you ain't the only one that ever gave me diamonds, Gus. You know that. I was wearin' a few when I met you.'

'I know,' he growled, 'but you wasn't wearin' these. Where'd you get them?'

'Here, pull in this corset, will you, Gus?' she said. 'Oh, them things I haven't worn in a long time. Kinda pretty, ain't they?'

Gus tugged at the strings which drew in the corset until Lil's waist was like a wasp's. Having completed the job, he grunted and sat down in a gilt chair which groaned under him.

'After I'm elected sheriff,' he said with a noticeable expansion of his chest, 'I'll get you a lot of rocks. Bigger than any you got, Lil. Then I'll be askin' somethin' of you.'

Lil looked puzzled.

'What's that, Gus? You don't mean – not gettin' married or anythin' like that. Things is all right as they are, ain't they?'

Jordan cleared his throat.

'Well, no it ain't that, Lil. Although, you know I'd marry you in a minute if you wanted it that way.'

'I don't,' said Lil.

'I tell you, Lil,' he went on, 'I'm gonna ask you to turn loose some o' them things you got in Chi. I don't know where you got them and I don't care a damn. But I'm plannin' for you to have nothin' I don't provide. See what I mean?'

Lil's eyes shot to her dressing-table and at the glitter there. She crossed to it and ran her hands through it all. In the glass she could see Jordan looking at the back of her head.

'You want me to sell all the rocks you ain't give me?' she demanded.

'Sure. I can't bear to see you wearin' anythin' else but my stuff. You know, Lil, you mean a lot to me. I want you to be a big success. Look, already since you been entertainin' downstairs we're doin' twice as much business as Nigger Mike Salter, or The Bucket of Blood. Why, everybody says you got it all over Della Fox. Even Tony Pastor's got his eye on you. Look at all them uptown swells that come down here now just to see Diamond Lil. Well, I want you to be just my Diamond Lil, and I just want you to have the diamonds I give you.'

'We'll talk about that when the time comes, Gus,' Lil said slowly. 'And I'm tellin' you now and tellin' you straight. Diamonds talk, and I can stand listenin' to 'em often.'

2

SUICIDE HALL

DIAMOND LIL finally succeeded in convincing Gus of the importance of getting to her photographer's before the sun was much higher.

Her bearded champion gave her a smacking kiss and, disappointed that there was to be no matinee, lumbered out of the boudoir. A moment later he could be heard bullying the porter, Steve, as a release for the energy Lil had forced him to retain.

Lil stepped into a blonde satin dress that hugged her corseted hips like the arms of a lover. A hat to match, with beige-coloured ostrich plumes, she perched jauntily over her pompadour. Then a long feather boa, also beige in colour, was gracefully draped about her lovely throat.

She studied herself in the mirror through long luxuriant lashes. 'Kid, you're class,' she told herself; then smiled, white teeth flashing. She hummed a few bars of 'Frankie and Johnny'. Quite casually her eyes were attracted to the diamond pendants concerning which Gus had been so perturbed.

The imp of the perverse bit her savagely, as he always did when Lil was told *not* to do a thing. She took one of the ear-drops and worked the hook through the lobe of her ear. 'Pretty!' she decided with a flourish of her head that made the pendant shimmer like the fragments of a shattered dream.

Then adjusting her remaining ear-drop, she snapped the catch and surveyed the completed effect. She found it very gorgeous indeed. And just because Gus Jordan had a dippy dislike for the glittering pendants she wasn't going to spoil that effect.

On her fingers and wrists was a profusion of other diamonds all calculated to blind the percipient male, who hesitated between sins of commission and omission, into thinking that fornication is a virtue.

Lil gave her flashing fingers a quick inventory and the check-up revealed one ring missing. This, a small stone set in a circle of imitation emeralds, she brought out from under a pile of paper money in the white and purple *bonheur du jour* that graced her dresser on a doily all its own. This shabby ring amidst its resplendent fellows was like a seedy anarchist at a Tammany banquet. But Lil wore it out of sentiment. She had taken it from the finger of a drunken lake-boat steward during hustling days in Chicago. He was hardly more than a boy and she could still remember how his auburn hair curled about his ears, and the honesty of his blue eyes. It had been her first diamond, and she had spat on it and kept it for luck.

Now as she drew on her long gloves her ears were assaulted by sounds which never failed to pain her and which she particularly detested. Down in the street beneath her window a Salvation Army group was exhorting sinners – pimps, prostitutes and stumblebums – to be made as little children and come to Jesus. The drums thumped with that unusually flat and dead detonation that somehow made one think of Heaven as an infinite flop-house where one's soul reclined eternally on lousy celestial mattresses. The trumpets only added to the impression.

Whenever Lil heard the holy howling, as she called it, she wondered why it was that saving one's soul was always made so dreary and unattractive, whereas the way to Hell was always so utterly delightful.

Although Lil's ears and nerves were tortured every time she heard the singing and playing of the soul-savers, she was constantly giving clothes and even money to the Salvation Army.

Today, as she looked from the window, and her eyes and mouth puckered in absolute distaste, she saw suddenly a tall square-shouldered young man, with dark, wavy hair, clad in the uniform of a captain. His face turned towards her window for an instant, and Lil noticed with increasing interest that he was handsome. Very handsome. Lil caught her breath and then let it out with a little hissing sound.

'Well,' she murmured after a moment, 'there's a good man wasted. He's the best-looking thing I've seen in a long time.'

Lil wondered what this Adonis was doing in that galaxy of sob-sisters. She didn't know much about the Salvation Army. She wondered if the young captain had to live like a priest since he was preaching religion. She knew that priests didn't marry. She speculated as to whether these Army men could or did. She was all at once curious to know if he was married.

She stared at the younger sisters of the Army who were in the group. She fixed penetrating eyes on the best-looking one, who was rather pretty, and she conjectured whether the handsome soldier of the Lord was wedded to her.

If he were not married, she argued further, then what did he do when he felt the need of a woman? Lil had no illusions concerning men. She knew them too well. If this young preacher yielded to his fleshly desires, how then did he square that up with denouncing those desires in others?

It was all very complex, and Lil decided she had better get on to her photographer's. As she looked down for the last time her eyes met his. The others were picking up drums, tambourines and trumpets, preparing to move on.

Lil's heart fluttered strangely for a moment and then she closed the window and went out of the room. She descended by the back stairs to the street, where old Mike, her coachman, rummy-nosed and already more than half cocked, waited with her hansom. Two smart grey geldings stood in the harness trying to chase the flies that settled on their flanks with braided and be-ribboned tails.

A passer-by's eye kindled voluptuously when he glimpsed Lil's trim ankles as she raised her skirts getting into the hansom, and he whistled softly to himself as he strolled down the street stroking the huge, black, pomaded moustache that ruled his face like the handle-bars on a bicycle.

Flounces and ruffles and feather boas . . . the sickish-sweet odour of cheap perfume mingled with the smell of Irish whisky . . . flying suds of mammoth schooners of beer . . . the hard bright faces of harlots . . . the bleared eyes and bloated faces of habitual drunkards . . . the bruised, swollen faces of rowdies and gangsters, killers, drug addicts . . . curses and smells and more curses . . . and underneath it all – crime, and the half-laughing, half-sneering face of lust . . .

That was Suicide Hall of the mauve and gay 'Nineties. That was Gus Jordan's little dancing hell in Chatham Square. In the alleys that led away from Gus's side-doors the pavement bore dark stains which no amount of scrubbing could obliterate. It looked like blood . . . and it was blood.

But Suicide Hall was just one of the joy-joints in the dump-heap out of which New York was beginning to rise. Immigrants, German, Irish, Italian, and Jews from Russia, Poland and the hidden ghettos of the world poured in through Castle Garden to be woven later into the fabric and to enrich the texture of New York.

Everywhere, it seemed there was an overwhelming pre-occupation with the frivolities. Downtown, virtue was only extolled in sentimental song when the night grew grey and tears came easily to fall saltily among the beer-slops. Up-town, vice was toyed with in a dandified way, a toothsome concomitant of lobster à la Newburg and champagne.

At Madison Square Garden the blue-bloods came to pin rosettes on equally blue-blooded horses, while in the bawdy-houses of Division Street gentlemen smelling of bay rum and whisky exchanged brass checks for the paid acrobatics of feminine flesh.

The Hoffman House bar does a land-office business and in Canal Street the sweatshops are labouring far into the night, pinched foreign faces hooked over their tasks . . . Julia Arthur is announced as 'The Supreme Bloom of Our National Beauty', and takes the critics by storm in *A Lady of Quality*, which endeavours to prove that the best way to terminate an adulterous affair is to brain one's love with a riding-crop . . . Down at Gravesend race-track a horse loses and a backer cuts his throat from ear to ear with a razor . . . At Koster & Bial's music-hall on Thirty-fourth Street dandies applaud the stamp and flutter of Carmencita, who exudes heat and temperament through corset and all. The ladies come veiled to see the cavortings of the dark señorita, a thing they do not do when they come to see Diamond Lil downstairs. In Suicide Hall they can comfortably put aside their veils along with less convenient inhibitions . . . and over and above all the Gibson Girl looks down with a chaste smile, and peaches and cream complexion . . .

Chatham Square began to come to life at noon. During the morning the Elevated above and pawnshop barkers below made a raucous din, but the pulse of the Square did not begin to throb until midday.

Then it filled suddenly, as if in response to some mysterious signal, with blue-shaven touts, small dive-keepers prowling for news of their competitors, and gambling-den steerers. Rooming-house flops came from the narrow street doorways to bat bleary eyes against the sun before starting the daily hunt among the barrel houses for eye-openers. Loose-lipped, pasty-faced pimps came up from the Bowery to check up with music-hall waiters on last night's earnings of their women.

Gus Jordan's saloon was one of the important resorts in the Square. Its colourful and rather awesome sobriquet, 'Suicide Hall', had grown out of the reprehensible habit prostitutes had of doing the Dutch act there when they had grown 'tired of it all'.

You went into Jordan's through the customary swinging doors, and you had your choice of leaning indolently against the brass-railed bar or proceeding to the back room, which also had a family entrance from the street. Here there was a collection of battle-scarred and booze-stained tables. In the centre was a cleared space where the entertainers for the clientele, mainly women, sang 'She's More To Be Pitied Than Censured', 'A Bird in a Gilded Cage', and other tear-jerkers that opened the hearts and the pocket-books of the listeners. The entertainers were not above hustling among the tables between turns. A stairway ascended from the room to a short balcony from which a door led into Lil's boudoir. It was from that door and down these stairs that Diamond Lil came when at the height of the evening Gus announced her as a special attraction from the floor below. And the way Lil descended those stairs, incandescent and scintillating amidst her diamonds, anyone will tell you was a caution.

This noon an open-mouthed group of habitués stood in front of the bar gazing with mixed emotions at the painting which adorned the back wall of the bar, and which was almost as long. The subject of the painting was none other than the alabaster and gold Lil reclining in all her voluptuous nudity upon a background of purple velvet. No masculine eye could travel from the crown of that spun-gold head past those vermilion-tipped peaks of breasts down to those curling rose-petal toes without being conscious of a physical change.

A visiting French artist had painted that lusty, life-like reproduction of Lil. The original had been sent to the World's

Fair in Chicago. Gus had had this copy made of it and he wanted to tell the world that Lil was his own especial property. Lil, as a matter of fact, had come into quite a demand as a model for illustrators since her début in Gus's place. Her picture was soon to be seen on new calendars, and already it appeared on the band of a high-priced cigar.

It was small wonder that the boys who clustered before the daring nude were flabbergasted at this unexpected view of Lil's charms which they all had thought were strictly reserved for Gus's private admiration.

'Phew!' exclaimed Chuck, pushing his curly-brimmed derby still farther over his right eye, and thrusting his hands into the pockets of his tight double-breasted jacket with the immense pearl buttons. 'Say, ain't dat a boid? S'help me Gawd, I ain't never seen a woman more beautifuller!' In his excitement he stuck the wrong end of his cigar in his mouth and began spitting out ashes.

'Yep,' said Bill the bartender, skilfully shooting a stream of brown tobacco-juice into a convenient gaboon. 'It just come this mornin'. Gus wouldn't eat his breakfast before he had it stuck up there.'

Spider Kane was staring at the picture intently. His jaw was clamped tightly and a muscle worked in one cheek. Then he quickly tossed off three-fingers of rye and wiped his mouth with the back of his hand. Kane was a bruiser and as hard as nails, but this picture did something to him.

Steak McGarry, singing waiter, grinned over his snaggle teeth and pointed an obscene finger.

'I'd like to make it an even once.'

'Let Gus hear you say dat,' snapped Chuck, 'an' you'll be pickin' lead out o' yer pants.'

Ragtime Kelly, lushing beer at the end of the bar, snickered.

'Oh, Steak has big ideas,' he asserted. 'You ain't gonna be a nickel-kicker all yer life, are yer, Steak?'

'Not wit' you playin' the pi-any for me,' Steak returned.

Spider Kane chewed a matchstick while his eyes continued to feast on Lil's exotic charms.

'Do it again,' he said to Bill, pushing his glass across the bar.

The swinging doors flapped like the ears on an elephant and immediately the group was conscious that a personality had entered the bar-room.

'Hello, Dan,' said Kane to the newcomer.

'Howdy, Flynn,' said Chuck.

'H'yer, boys?' greeted Dan Flynn as he came up to the bar.

Flynn was sartorially resplendent. His long, lean frame was encased in a dove-grey Prince Albert coat, a double-breasted waistcoat of cream brocade, striped trousers and pearl-grey derby with spats to match. A heavy gold chain spanned his chest. He was a politician and gambler, sharp-eyed, shrewd, self-possessed, as ambitious as Cæsar. He had risen by devious ways from the underworld, but his origin was veneered by a superficial polish.

He raised an eyebrow as the huge picture of Lil loomed before his eyes. He whistled.

'So that's Diamond Lil?' he stated rather than asked.

'Where you been?' inquired Steak McGarry. 'We ain't seen you in here in a hell of a while.'

Flynn smiled expansively. His eyes did not leave the enticing Lil.

'Well, boys, the drinks are on me. Set 'em up, Bill. Yes, I been away, but I'm figurin' on bein' around from now on.'

3

JUST ANOTHER SALLY

AFTER Dan Flynn had bought a couple of rounds of drinks to show what a great fellow he was, he casually touched Spider Kane on the arm and nodded his head in the direction of the back room.

'I want to talk private to you, Kane,' Flynn said out of the corner of his mouth.

Kane tossed off his drink and strode out of the bar. Flynn swaggered after him.

Dan Flynn's ambitions to become a Bowery power were well known, but he had neither the following nor the points of contact that Gus Jordan possessed, so his efforts up to date to achieve any real political influence were abortive.

He did, however, have certain favourable – for himself – connections with the Police Department. He had organized a bunch of petty thieves and secured from the police the pickpocket privileges at the Manhattan terminal of the Brooklyn Bridge. This was a steady source of income. He paid off the police officials under whose protection his crooks operated, and took as his share an excellent cut of the ill-gotten gains.

Flynn had also tipped off the cops on occasions when he thought the turning up of a crook would redound to his benefit.

Spider Kane played a little shut-eye with him once in a while. Kane knew every woman on the pavements and those who circulated among the dives, from Park Row to Chatham Square; from the frowses of the Five Points cellar dumps to the garbage-can maggots of Mulberry Bend.

It was his business to spot every new girl exploring the easiest way, and find out who the man was behind her to whom she gave her earnings. If she was on her own he quickly made her understand that wouldn't do. She'd have to get a man to sponsor her who would kick in for her to Dan Flynn. If she proved stubborn she was either given a lacing or run in, sometimes both. If she complied she was a member of good standing as the saying goes, and she could hustle to her heart's content but part of her earnings had to wind up in Flynn's pocket. In return Flynn fronted for her when the police interfered.

Flynn and Kane had hardly settled themselves in the back room before Steak McGarry, loud-mouthed and facetious, trailed in, followed by Chuck and Ragtime Kelly. The latter immediately seated himself at the piano and began to pound away.

Flynn snorted in disgust.

'Come on back inside,' he said to Kane, and murmured something more about 'these blasted bar-flies'.

'They ain't bar-flies, Dan,' said Kane. 'Chuck is on the inside with Gus. Don't you forgit that.'

Flynn grunted.

'I ain't forgettin' it. I'm just beginnin' to remember it.'

They started back to the bar. Kelly was tearing the notes of 'Silver Threads Among the Gold'.

Chuck turned to him with a sour look.

'Wot's dat yer playin'?' he demanded of Kelly.

'It says the floosies don't count when it comes to yer old woman,' Ragtime explained.

'Dere ain't no sense to dat,' Chuck protested.

18

In the bar Bill set up drinks for Flynn and Kane as they draped themselves over one end of the mahogany.

Flynn nodded curtly to the other room.

'See what the boys in the back room'll have,' he ordered. 'And for cripes' sake keep 'em in there!'

For a moment Flynn and his companion studied the recumbent Lil in her gilt frame over the bar. She dominated the bar and the music-hall beyond as completely and arrogantly as she dominated Gus's bedroom upstairs.

'Gus ain't keepin' none of his secrets,' Spider observed reflectively. Flynn made no reply. He still studied the nude vision with a somewhat detached gaze, as if he were thoughtful. Spider remarked: 'Them legs o' Lil's is got more class than Della Fox's and Pauline Hall's put together.'

Flynn gulped his whisky without breaking his gaze at the dazzling woman on the canvas. Spider sipped his beer and looked over the rim of his glass at fresh details of the undraped figure. 'Now there's a bust for you, ain't it?' he murmured, half to himself. Suddenly he put down his glass sharply and clutched at his companion's arm, stirred by an abrupt discovery.

'Look, Flynn, at the rocks around her neck and on her hands? She's lousy with 'em!'

Flynn gave him a withering look. 'You got that far up at last, did you? What you been doin'? Imagining?'

'Well, whatdaya expect? Can you look at a dame all showin' like that an' not go thinkin' things? Don't stand to reason. An' if you ast me I'm sayin' that's what Jordan put her up there for.'

The booming voice of Jordan was heard. Gus had no liking for Flynn, but he had risen from a small side-street saloon to his present prominence by being genial when there was no reason to be otherwise.

'Hello, Flynn,' he greeted his visitor, slapping him on the back heartily. 'Good old Dan Flynn! Ain't seen you in my place in over a month. Where you been?'

19

'Here, there, and everywhere, Gus. Town's getting so damn big these days it takes time to travel over it. I'll bet one of these days we'll be walking over a bridge to Long Island.'

'Walkin'? Say, Dan, we'll be riding over to Long Island, in one of them new horseless buggies.'

'Think so?'

'I know so. This here city's goin' to lead the world one of these days. We've got everything to build on and we've got brainy men like me to do the building.'

'You're a brainy man, Gus. Got to say that for you. But about those horseless buggies – I don't know!'

'What I know about 'em is that I'm going to buy one for me and Lil. What'll you have, Dan? An' you, Kane?'

Flynn acknowledged the whisky. Steve sat up. 'Think you'll be elected, Dan?'

'I'm nominated, ain't I?' Gus puffed out his chest and stuck his thumbs in the armholes of his waistcoat. 'That's good as bein' elected. But bein' sheriff of this here county ain't goin' to be so easy. Puttin' people out of their homes and that kind of thing is hard.'

'That's a lot better, just the same, than puttin' people in homes that ain't good for 'em.' Flynn spoke with barely disguised meaning. Jordan flushed with quick anger. There were plenty of rumours that he was the biggest of the white slave traffickers, but he allowed nobody to face him with even a hint of their truth.

'What do you mean by that, Flynn?'

Flynn hedged quickly and suavely. 'Oh, I mean like having to do with the cops, puttin' women in gaol and making them spill the sob stuff.'

'Oh, that's it, hey? I thought you might be meaning something else.'

'I wouldn't mean anything else, Gus. Don't get hot under the collar. Say, that's a swell paintin' you got up there. How's Lil, anyway?'

'She's all right, and what's more she's satisfied.'

'She ought to be.' Flynn's tone was flattering. Jordan was mollified and waved to Steve to replenish the whisky glasses and Spider Kane's schooner. 'She's sure a handsome dame,' Flynn went on. 'I'd think you'd be jealous. There's lots of men who'd like to get her away from you.'

Jordan drank slowly before he replied. He looked up at the canvas, moving his glance from the half-curled toes of Lil's bare feet to the blonde splendour of her unbound hair. 'I admit,' he said when he put down his glass, 'that I do get sort o' mad when some of the boys get too forward with her. But she knows how to handle 'em. Lil ain't all mush, like some dames. An' it's pretty nice to have a girl like her that can take her pick and all the men are after. Show's I'm up to scratch, eh? And look at this, Flynn,' he added, taking out a plush-covered box and snapping it open to reveal a huge solitaire that almost blinded Flynn. 'Ain't it a pip?'

'Phew!' whistled Flynn. 'It's a beaut'. Must've set you back a pretty penny, Gus.'

'Oh,' said Gus airily, 'fifteen hundred. But Lil's worth it. There ain't nothin' too good for my Lil.'

Ragtime Kelly finished playing, 'She May Have Seen Better Days', with a heart-wrenching flourish and Steak McGarry came into the bar.

'That thing Ragtime was playin' started a jane off at one of the tables,' Steak reported to Jordan. 'She looks like a piece of junk to me, an' we already had one of them things this mornin'. Shall I t'row her out, Boss?'

Jordan went to the bar-room door and looked into the music-hall.

'Over there in the corner,' Steak pointed.

The girl Steak indicated was young, with an almost doll-like face framed in blonde curls. She had chosen a table in a far corner of the hall, darkened by shadows. She had thrown down her hat and slumped into a chair. She wore a dark shoulder-cape over a cheap voile dress. Her eyes were closed as if the tune Ragtime had played evoked visions, and her body was shaking with dry, choked-off sobs.

'When did she come in?' Gus asked Steak. 'Do you know her?'

'Never seen her in here before. She slunk in when I wasn't lookin'. Musta been while you was in your office. I been watchin' her an' when she begins to whine I know the signs.'

'Probably dodging the bulls,' Flynn observed, and Spider Kane made a move to go over to her.

'I ain't seen her no place,' Spider said, with ready realization that here was a jane on the make he didn't have on his collection list. Probably didn't have a pimp, or had been thrown out by one she did have. In either event he'd take her in hand and turn her over to somebody who'd keep her working instead of sitting around a joint wasting her time whining. 'I'll get her out o' here,' he said.

Jordan caught him by the shoulder and thrust him aside. 'This is my place, Kane. What comes in my door, I'll take care of. She don't look like a regular to me.'

Spider shrugged his shoulders in disgust behind Jordan's back as the latter approached the table where the girl with the curly hair sat with her eyes closed and her sobs racking her shoulders. Flynn lit a fresh cigar and watched.

Jordan laid a hand on the girl's arm. 'What's the matter with you? Are you in trouble?'

The girl opened her eyes and lifted her face to look into his. Her eyes were dark pools of ineffable tragedy. On her cheeks were the traces of tears that had dried. Barely more than seventeen, Jordan thought. Nothing of dope or dissipation in her young face. Though she looked into Jordan's eyes, she seemed not to see him. Her head dropped suddenly into her arms and her sobs were released.

'It's more – more than just trouble,' she moaned, her voice muffled in her arms.

Ragtime began to thump a new tune, picking it out laboriously from a new sheet of music labelled 'Hearts and Flowers'. Jordan was annoyed.

'Cut that out!' he shouted at the piano-player. 'Get out of here and cool off.'

Ragtime got off his stool hastily, gathered his music and hurried into the bar, out of Jordan's sight. Gus shook the girl's shoulder.

'Come on, now. Tell me what's wrong. Maybe I can help you.'

Flynn strolled close to the table and took his cigar out of his mouth. He appraised the girl with a keen glance, noting the youthful contours of her body under the cheap dress, and bent to catch a glimpse of her face, half-hidden in her arms. 'Better lay off, Gus,' he said. 'Better let Spider have her. You ain't used to them kind.'

Jordan turned on him brusquely. 'What I told Spider goes for you too, Flynn.' Dan refused to take offence but stepped back to lean over a chair and watch the scene. Jordan spoke to the girl again. 'I'll help you if you'll tell me what's the matter.'

The girl stirred, lifting her head. 'Oh, I can't! I can't tell you. I – I couldn't tell anyone.'

'Why not? There ain't nothin' you can't tell.'

The girl shook her head slowly, hopelessly. She still leaned across the table, her head down, staring at the floor, but unseeing. In her voice was the despair that only youth can feel and only once in a lifetime – the first time!

'It's – it's too – terrible! I – I couldn't even tell – anybody.'

Flynn's lip curled contemptuously. 'Janes that weep is always bad business, Gus,' he said. 'I'm warning you for your own good.'

Gus gave him no reply, but snapped his fingers at Bill who

was emerging from the bar with a tray of drinks for a group of customers that had drifted in from the Square. From the tray Jordan chose a glass of brandy. He held the glass close to the girl's outstretched hand.

'Here. Drink this. It'll make you see things different like.'

'Please, Mister! I don't want anything to drink. I – I couldn't!'

Spider Kane, who had remained close to his boss, whispered to Flynn out of the corner of his mouth: 'You tell by the way she talks she ain't a regular tart. She's out of a family. Been tryin' somethin' that's too tough for 'er.'

Jordan put the drink on to the table. 'Well, if you don't want a drink, do you know what in th' hell you do want?'

This time the girl looked up again. Her mouth, that should have been naturally red, was drained of every vestige of colour. 'I know,' she said slowly. 'I want – to – die!'

Flynn laughed shortly. 'She's come to the right place all right, eh, Gus?'

Jordan wheeled round, flushed and belligerent. 'What do you mean by that, Flynn?'

Flynn affected blank astonishment that Jordan should be peeved. 'Why, I understand from the boys that you have sometimes as much as a dozen kick-offs here in a week. They call your place Suicide Hall, don't they? The skirts know where to come, don't they?'

'If you don't like my place get out of it.' Jordan squared his bulky shoulders as if he prepared, or was ready, to be his own bouncer. Spider Kane moved backwards ready to make for the street door. He'd serve Dan Flynn in any kind of crooked deal, but he saw no sense in being part of a showdown with Gus Jordan. But Flynn drew in his oars 'Take a joke, Gus,' he said, with a wave of his cigar. 'Take a joke.'

'Some jokes I don't take,' Jordan snapped, and returned to the girl, who had again dropped her head on to the table. 'What's your name?'

The girl's whisper rose past her shoulder. 'It's – it's just "Sally".'

Jordan gazed down at the back of the girl's head. He thrust his hands into his pocket and was uncomfortable. Five minutes later, when Sally was out of sight with her racking sobs and all the centuries of Eve's torture in her wide blue eyes and about her quivering mouth, he would send for the Chinese, Charlie Fong, who kept a dingy, strong-barred trap in Mott Street for the eager little moths Gus sent to have their wings singed in the pink-curtained vice world of Rio. And he would tell Charlie that maybe he'd have a new one for the trap, a particularly pretty one with the yellow hair the South Americans liked, and who ought to bring an extra thousand dollars. He'd tell Charlie to have the trap ready, and the Chinese would bob gleefully in anticipation. But just now, Sally was there before him, her head down, crying, and was very pathetic and heart-touching.

Gus's heart was easily touched, if you were close enough to him to reach out for it. If only Spider Kane had found Sally in some other place, and had taken her into a back room, locked the door and then beat her until she was black and blue all over and ready to turn herself and her two-dollar street fees over to any man he should name, Spider might have come into Jordan's place and told Gus all about his new pick-up, and Gus would have been cold. What's a woman for, anyway? An' what can she expect? If she's got brains she out-smarts the pimps, like Lil, for example. If she ain't got brains, what the hell?

Gus Jordans are not rare in the world. They are the opposite type from, say, prosecuting attorneys who will deliberately send innocent men to the gallows for a few newspaper headlines. Gus wouldn't have had the heart to send a girl to Rio if she discovered what she was going into and pleaded with him to spare her. He would have paid

Charlie Fong for the trouble of trapping her, put money in her purse and sent her home.

So Sally's trouble, whatever it was, worried him. Not because of itself, whatever it was, but because it brought her into his place and to one of his tables. 'If you don't want a drink, and don't want to talk to nobody, what did you come in here for?' he asked her sharply.

The girl got up, wearily, and steadied herself against her chair. 'I don't know. Oh, I don't know. I'll go if I'm in the way.'

Jordan caught her arm and braced her. 'Here! You can't go out the way you are. You stay here and I'll take care of you. You'll tell me what's the matter after a while and maybe I can help.'

She looked at him with gratitude none the less impulsive and sincere for all of her abject hopelessness. He led her through the bar-room to an inner room just large enough for a round table, two chairs and a commodious settee.

'You go in here and pull yourself together. I'll send in a drink. You drink it.'

'Nobody can help me.'

'You take your drink when it comes and you'll think different.'

He closed the door to the little room and stopped at the bar to order whisky sent in and left on the table. 'When you go in,' he ordered Steve, 'look her over. If you think she's got anything, poison, you keep watch.'

He stood at the bar a moment and drained a drink for himself. When Steve came out from the inner room he remarked:

'She's a looker, Boss, for them as likes 'em dainty. Some prefers 'em without too much meat.'

Jordan studied his empty glass silently. His tenderness over the girl's anguish and whatever had caused it began to recede. She was out of sight. He returned to the outer hall and saw that Dan Flynn was talking with Chuck. When Chuck saw him he left Flynn and walked over.

Jordan jerked his head backward, indicating the room off the bar.

'What do you think, Chuck?'

'You mean Charlie Fong? She'd make a nice piece of goods.'

4

THE MAN FROM RIO

DIAMOND LIL was rather proud of the pictures that the photographer turned over to her. They showed her off to her best advantage. Some of them even more than her best advantage. The latter, Lil, who was something of an exhibitionist, expected to use to titillate the souls of the men who came to Gus's and admired her but dared not touch her, but who would be more grateful for a peep at the charms which Gus had been careful to let all and sundry know were his exclusively. These pictures were not pornographic, to make a fine point of it, but they were *risqué*, or, as the word went – 'daring'.

Old Mike, who had been bending the merry elbow in a saloon at the corner, had already climbed to his perch by the time Lil came out of the photographer's, for he was a little shaky on his pins and dreaded the invective Lil might pour on his dirty grey poll, if she found him stewed to the gills.

'You're a hell of a coachman,' Lil said, when she saw him. 'Why aren't you down here to help me in?'

'Sure, an' I'm sorry, ma'am,' Mike whined. 'I'll be there the nex' time.'

Lil smiled to herself. She knew what ailed the old soak, but she felt she had to check up on him once in a while so he wouldn't think he was getting away with anything on her.

Mike steered the hansom down Broadway, and then swerved over through East Houston Street to the Bowery. As they arrived at Grand Street, Lil heard the pulsing of drums and the strident blare of trumpets, and she knew that the Salvation Army was in the immediate vicinity. She called to Mike to halt.

'What is it, ma'am?' Mike wanted to know.

'Where's that music comin' from?' Lil inquired.

''Pears like it might be comin' from Elizabeth Street, around the corner from Grand,' responded Mike, cocking one ear to windward.

'Drive around there and find out,' Lil ordered.

'What the hell?' thought Mike, but he gee'd at the horses and did as he had been commanded.

As a matter of fact, Lil almost wondered. 'What the hell?' herself. She did not exactly know what the something was that made her want to draw near the music of the Army, which was always so painful to her. Nevertheless, she did not conceal from herself that somehow she would be pleased if she got another look at the young captain. She hoped he would be with this group.

The young captain was indeed in the group, and Lil, sitting back in the shadow of her hansom, gave Mike the word to pull up. She peered through the little side window and was forced to admit that the good captain was really as handsome as he had appeared on first inspection.

She liked his manly carriage. The attitude of self-containment. He stood firmly on his two feet, and there was a determined look about his jaw. In other words, Lil told herself that he looked as if he had 'guts'.

Gus had guts, too, and besides the fact that he could give her acres of diamonds, she admired that nerve in him which had lifted him from an ordinary saloon keeper to a prominent politician.

She was quite pleased that this second glance at the

captain showed him to be all man and not just a wishy-washy psalm-singer.

Lil watched until the group had packed up and moved on. Then with a slight sigh, which she could not explain to herself, Lil woke up Mike with a few choice words, and got him started back home.

As a rule she entered the bar-room and dance-hall on her return from shopping excursions, but today, which was extremely warm, she had a slight headache and decided to go to her room by the back way and freshen her body with eau-de-Cologne. Mike she instructed to take her packages which she had managed to acquire on her way to the photographer's despite the hurry she had professed about getting there early, and inform Gus that she would be indisposed for a little while.

'Where's Lil?' Gus wanted to know, when Mike staggered in with the packages.

Mike described her indisposition as:

'Miss Lil ain't feelin' good. Guess it's the heat. She went right to her room, but she says as how she'll be down if not sooner then later.'

Flynn, whom Gus was finding very boring, laughed.

'Well, Gus, I shouldn't think Lil'd mind the heat.'

'I guess not. Accordin' to your manner of thinkin', Flynn,' Gus returned.

Flynn stared at him.

Gus had another reason besides boredom for wanting Flynn out of his place. He was expecting Rita. Rita Christinia, concerning whom Gus had received word that she had arrived from Rio. Gus had some business to transact with Rita. It was to be of a very private nature, as all of Gus's business with Rita chanced to be, and he did not want Flynn to be privy to any of it.

'It's a marvel to me, Flynn,' Gus remarked pointedly, 'that a busy man like you has time to hang around a place like this. Specially when you ain't in the business.'

Flynn hung a long thumb in the armhole of his waistcoat and studied his cigar.

'Well, for one thing, Gus,' he declared, 'I like your brand of liquor. Second, I like you. And third, I'm takin' the day off. Any objections?'

'And fourth,' Gus said with scarcely veiled sarcasm, 'you're dyin' to see Lil, eh?'

'Well, now, Gus,' replied Flynn, 'I'm ashamed of myself for overlookin' that point. You sure hit the nail on the head.'

'I warn you,' asserted Gus, 'when you see Lil, you'll envy me the rest of your days, Flynn.'

'I envy you already, Gus,' answered Flynn with more truth than poetry. He rose and stretched himself. 'I'm goin' into the bar, Gus, and drink some of your whisky and look at your Lil in the picture, till I can see her for real. Will you join me?'

'I'll be in in a minute,' said Gus, glad of the opportunity for a breathing-space away from the self-assured Flynn.

Flynn swaggered out, the doors flapping behind him.

Jordan bit savagely into a fresh cigar, and paced up and down. He glanced up the stairs towards Lil's room, crossed over to the little room and peered in at woebegone Sally who by now apparently had sobbed herself to sleep. Her head was in her arms and she was breathing quietly. Gus drew a sigh of relief. For an instant he thought she might have done the Dutch act. He was getting a little bit sick of having his place dubbed Suicide Hall. That sort of stuff was getting to be a little bit too sticky for a man who was to be the next sheriff, and God knows what else afterward.

He hoped now that Rita would stay away until after Flynn had gone.

Rita Christinia was Gus's liaison officer with the flesh marts of Brazil and the Argentine. Rita had had a remarkable training both in selling and buying on the hoof of the kind of maidens fair that made a very profitable investment for the bordellos of South America. Young women from the United

States were very much in favour in the stockades of Rio de Janeiro and other convenient port cities of the southern continent. Rita, because of her business acumen, had risen from a passion flower herself to her present affluent position.

She was a thorough Latin, dark, vivacious, volcanic of passions and sadistic. Above all, she was a typical Madame, with a heart as cold as a polar bear's kiss. She hated Lil. Was intensely jealous of her. How she would have loved to have seen Lil on her way to the brothels of Rio! How she would have liked to lash Lil's white flesh with a cat-o'-nine-tails, as she had lashed so many of her charges who had proved the least bit recalcitrant. Rita had cruelly beaten to death more than one girl who had refused to be broken when she learned her destination.

She had come to New York four years before, and had returned four times a year since. She had wanted to establish a good contact in the States. Charlie Fong, the sleek little almond-eyed merchant of Mott Street, had paved the way for her. He had interested Gus Jordan. Jordan at first couldn't see that kind of thing. It was too dirty; but after he had been persuaded to make one shipment of damsels he discovered that dirty money had the same power as clean. Some of the money he gave to the Salvation Army and to neighbouring churches to salve his conscience. Thus he believed that though his sins be scarlet they would be washed as white as snow on Doomsday.

Gus and Rita had laid their plans carefully. They could, of course, have enlisted the services of a corps of touts who would find good-looking girls among the tenements, make love to them, and ship them to South America on any one of a dozen tried-out pretexts. Rita could meet them there and 'break' them. But this process involved an expensive organization, money split too many ways And there was another drawback. The girl, arriving in Rio, might still be in love. She would have to suffer not only her breaking, but her disillusionment. Sometimes their health gave way under the forlornness of their sentimental agonies. They had to be nursed and catered to, or their bodies would deteriorate. They were, in short, too much trouble.

Better to find those who were free from entanglements. Already fallen, but not yet on the streets. And without families that would raise too much of a row when they disappeared. This kind could be lured with promises of various kinds of jobs. And once in Rita's hands, in a strange city among a strange people, they could soon be made to listen to reason, such as it was.

Gus found that kind with the help of Charles Fong, who kept them in his Mott Street trap until Rita came for them. Sometimes Rita took back with her as many as twenty girls, and always sent Gus from four hundred to six hundred dollars a head for them, after she sold them. And Rita knew where to sell them to get the biggest price. She never took less than a thousand a head. A good girl could earn up to fifty thousand dollars for her house before she was ready for the ash-bin or a mosquito swamp.

Gus suddenly ceased perambulating the back room of his saloon, for all at once appeared the very person who was uppermost in his mind at the moment. None other than the slimy Rita.

She swished in from the family entrance, and the odour of chypre accompanied her.

'Good old Rita!' Gus exclaimed. 'I'd heard you was in, but wasn't sure. When'd you hit town?'

She gave him both of her gloved hands and flashed him a gay smile. A gold molar helped to make it especially brilliant.

'It is but yesterday, one day ago. The land, it is glad to my feet. One day I wait, then I come to you.'

'Fine. That's fine. Glad you're here. Me and Charlie are all ready. Have a good trip?'

She threw up her expressive hands. 'Pretty nice. But eet was not all nice. We would 'ave arrive five day ago, but the ship, she is 'ave trouble near Trinidad. We mus' wait there.'

'We?' Gus echoed. For the first time he took note that Rita had not entered alone. His suspicious eyes fastened themselves on a man who bore all the earmarks of a South American. Tall, swarthy, and young, Rita's companion gave an appearance of sleekness. The dark hair on his head was as smooth as a seal's, and the slightest sort of a moustache graced the upper lip of his handsome Latin face. He was faultlessly groomed, and he bore himself with a jaunty and indifferent air. To Gus, he didn't appear to be much of a man. Too much of the dandy about him, but Gus was forced to admit that the South American no doubt was something for the ladies. He looked as though he could whisper just the right things into shell-pink ears; and with a convincing touch that only a professional in the art of love-making could successfully exploit.

Gus frowned in annoyance. Then quickly framed a laugh. 'A friend, Rita?'

Rita gave that musical laugh of hers which always sounded so genuine because it was so artistically false.

'Oh, but I forget all about Pablo.' She reached her fingers to him.

The man, with an easy, graceful movement, came to her side. She introduced him then to Jordan.

'This is Pablo Juarez. In Rio he is what you call of great fame. He is the youngest toreador. I make him — ' She turned to him with a quick smile which was in itself an answer to the question she asked him. 'What is it I shall say of you, my Pablo?'

He bowed to her with a lithe grace. 'Have we not agreed upon the word? Assistant?'

'Si, si! That is it. I make him my assistant. I am no longer lonesome with such a nice assistant. Now tell me, Gus, how is the so beautiful Diamond Lil, eh?'

'She's fine, Rita. Same's she always is. She's up in her room, but she'll be down before long. She'll be glad to see you.'

Gus and Rita's conversation had floated in bits into the bar-room beyond, and Flynn's attention was drawn away from the life-like painting of Lil. He recognized Rita's imperfect English, for he had met her once before. Her arrival told him that something was afoot. He had been hoping for just such a happening as this. He had suspected long that Rita and Gus were hand-in-glove in some kind of chicanery. He had a suspicion that it was white slavery. But he wasn't sure. If he was sure – well, then Flynn would not have dawdled, he would have gone into action.

He knew that Gus would resent his barging in at that moment, but because he had more or less set himself out to annoy Gus and worry him, he was glad of the opportunity.

He strutted through the swinging doors.

Gus immediately interrupted what he was saying to Rita, with a snort of irritation. Then controlling his feelings, he said with an effort at sociability:

'Oh, Rita, this is Dan Flynn. You remember him.'

Rita remembered Flynn vaguely, but gave him her hand with a show of delighted recognition, and veiled her eyes slumbrously. You could never tell what man might be useful, nor when.

'Flynn,' Gus went on, 'this is Mr. Jawrez, a friend of Rita's.'

'No, no!' protested Pablo. 'Juarez!'

Flynn ran a shrewd eye over Pablo, then smiled and extended his hand.

'What's your name again? Foreign names ain't any easier for me than they are for Gus.'

Pablo bowed slightly and slid a hand into his breast-pocket.

'I am Señor Pablo Phillippe Martay Juarez. My card.'

He produced the bit of pasteboard and offered it to Flynn.

'Well, I'm glad to know you, Mr. Juarez,' said Flynn,

pocketing the card for future reference. He turned to Gus, who was talking in low tones with Rita.

'Lil ain't met Mr. Juarez yet, has she, Gus?'

'Not Yet,' Gus snapped.

Rita's eyes narrowed at Flynn's words, more particularly at the manner in which he spoke them.

Flynn noticed the effect of his word on Rita.

'Well,' he declared with a broad smile, swinging around to Pablo, 'you've certainly got a treat in store for you, Mr. Juarez. All the men around here are nutty about Lil.'

'What is that "nuts"?' Juarez inquired, a bit bewildered.

'You'll find out,' said Flynn. 'Come on inside and I'll show you Lil's pitcher.'

He ushered Pablo towards the bar. Rita made as if to stop her companion, but Gus motioned her to let them go.

As they passed through the swinging doors Pablo caught sight of the huge canvas behind the bar. The rhythm of white flesh that was Lil smote him full in the face.

'Sacramento!' exploded Señor Pablo Phillippe Martay Juarez.

5

LIL LOOKS IT OVER

WHILE Flynn was entertaining Pablo Juarez in the bar, and telling him all he knew about Lil's ways with men, and while Pablo was feasting his eyes on Lil's picture with a growing fire inside of him, Gus had drinks brought for himself and Rita and sat with her at a table out of earshot of the bar.

'You're sure this fellow Jawrez is all right?' Gus asked gruffly, jerking his head towards the outer room.

'Juarez, Gus,' Rita corrected 'It is spel' with a "J"; but you do not say the "J". You say it like "W". Warez, like.'

Gus grunted. 'Well, whatever it is, I'm asking you can you vouch for him?'

'But of course,' Rita asserted. 'You know I am the good business woman, Gus. Would I bring him here if he was not all right?'

'Well, if you say so,' Gus replied doubtfully. Then his face suddenly brightened. He glanced toward the bar and then back to Rita. 'By the way, Rita.'

'Yes?'

He jabbed his thumb in the direction of the side room. 'Go in there,' he said, 'and open the door on your left. There's a kid in there. Take a squint at her. Tell her you busted in by mistake, and come out.'

Rita gave him a lift of her eyebrows and rose from the table. She crossed the dance-hall and entered the side room.

As soon as Rita had gone, Gus stepped to the swinging doors of the bar and called:

'Chuck!'

'Comin', Boss!' Chuck's voice came back to him.

The short, stocky figure of his trusted lieutenant a moment later entered, derby and cigar cocked at right-angles to each other.

'Say, Boss,' Chuck said, 'who is dat boid in dere wit' do moniker a coupla yards long? A greaser, ain't he?'

'Yeah!' Gus replied with a grin. 'Don't any of you boys get rough with him.'

'Gawd, Boss,' Chuck said, jerking the cigar from his mouth, 'he's lookin' at Lil's pitcher like he'd like to eat it. But if yer say we ain't to slug him, we'll let him git by.'

'Don't pay any attention to him,' Gus ordered. 'Now listen, Chuck, go over and tell Charlie Fong I want to see him in my office right away.'

Chuck nodded and went out without further ado.

Rita in the meantime had opened the door to the room where Sally was. The girl had dropped on to the floor and bowed her head on her arms, which she had flung across the cushions of the settee. She looked up when Rita entered and dragged herself to her feet.

'Oh, I take the wrong door,' Rita said, with an ingratiating smile.

Her eyes quickly ticked off for her the various points of the girl's appearance, her gaze lingering on Sally's blonde hair.

'If you want to come in, I'll go,' Sally said, reaching for her pathetic little bonnet.

'No, no, please,' Rita said smoothly. 'I am sorry to intrude. I make mistake. Mr Jordan, he say you stay here, is it not so?'

'I don't know his name,' murmured Sally. 'A big bearded man kindly said I could rest here.'

'Oh, yes, that is Mr. Jordan. He is ver' kind, ver nice man. You are ver' wise to trust him, if he wish to help you.'

'Thank you,' said Sally demurely. 'I – I don't know what I am to do.'

'Then take his advice. Excuse me, I go now.'

Rita found Gus waiting, twirling a whisky-glass between his fingers. She nodded to him silently, and sat down at the table.

'Charlie will be coming over later,' Gus said. 'But she'll be a hard one to handle. She's young, and she's as timid as a rabbit. She'll have to be treated with kid gloves.'

'Why do you not let your Lil handle her?' said Rita, just as though it were a brand new idea with her.

Gus shook her head.

'I don't want Lil mixed up in this thing of ours, now or any time.'

Rita's eyes flashed angrily, but she conquered her sudden temper.

'Ah, so it is that, eh? The lady of the heart, she is too precious? Then I will do it.'

She moved as if to go at once and talk to Sally with the honeyed promises of the serpent in Eden. Jordan stopped her.

'Wait a minute, Rita. It won't do for you to handle her.'

'And why not, Gus?' Rita snapped frigidly.

'Because we gotta be careful. You ain't seen around here much. If it got known that you had anything to do with her, and then it was found out that you was missin' and she was missin', some goddam snoopin' bastard would put two and two together and there'd be hell to pay. We gotta be damn careful. I been warned.'

'Warned?' Rita echoed. 'What do you mean?'

She was immediately anxious. Her wide eyes narrowed. Her fingers gripped Jordan's arm. 'What, Gus? What you hear? Tell me. I do not desire trouble. I have got my Pablo to t'ink about.'

Gus snorted.

'Hell, losin' that guy wouldn't be nothin' to cry over, would it? Can't see what you want with bedroom furniture like him.' He stopped abruptly and leaned forward, and he laid his hand down on the table flatly and firmly. 'I don't care a sneeze in hell about him. I'm thinkin' of my own skin. A lot of uptown silk stockin's is sittin' on the mayor an' I'm warned the police is watchin' me an' this place. Put a flat-foot on the job that's one of them kind you can't make listen to reason. Besides, I'm runnin' for sheriff of this here county. If they get me in this, I'm finished here and I'm finished in politics. Get me?'

'But how can they know anything? How can they suspect?' Rita demanded.

'I don't know,' Gus asserted. 'By God, I wish I did. But they got suspicions somehow, and like I say I'm bein' watched.'

'How do you know this?' – anxiously.

'One of my regular girls, Flo. You'll remember her. Got it from a stool what used to be her pimp.'

Rita looked into Gus's eyes. And then shook a finger slowly.

'Then it is that Lil should do something with the girl inside. No one ever suspect Diamond Lil. She is so grand. An' listen, Gus, Lil need not know what for she does this. Lil has good heart. She will be helping this girl, do you not see?'

Gus smiled cynically.

'Helping her to hell.'

'Ah, hell!' Rita sniffed. 'You do not believe that nonsense. Hell is what you make for yourself.'

'Well,' said Gus grudgingly, 'I'll see what Lil says about this dame. If she wants to help her, all right, I won't press her too hard.'

'As you will,' said Rita with a shrug. She had won her point. 'When are we to see the pretty little birds Charlie Fong got in cage?'

'When Charlie comes over I'll ask him.' The sound of a door opening upstairs made him look up. He rose.

'Here's Lil, now.'

It was Lil who moved languidly out on the balcony and came leisurely down the stairs. She had not changed the dress she had worn to the photographer's. Her lips parted in a dazzling smile as she saw Rita; not that she cared anything for the Latin woman, but secretly suspected her of being the bitch she was; still, Lil, unless crossed, was pleasant to everyone.

Rita crossed swiftly to Lil and had her hand before she had descended from the last step.

'Lil!' Rita cried. 'I am so happy to see you. You are even more beautiful than when last I see you!'

'Hello, Rita,' Lil said casually. 'Whenja get in?'

'Oh, one, two day ago!'

'Well, make yerself at home,' Lil invited.

At the sound of Lil's voice the swinging doors to the bar were held open by the crowd therein, eager to get a look at the voluptuous Lil, who seemed to flow rather than walk across the floor, her hips moving with a rhythmic sway that whetted their sensual appetites.

Flynn immediately burst through the crowd, followed by Juarez, who was almost panting with excitement.

'Hello, Lil!' Flynn said heartily.

'Well, Flynn,' Lil answered, really surprised at seeing him. 'Where you been? I ain't seen you around.'

'Been kinda busy, Lil. Kinda busy. You're lookin' great.'

'Thanks,' said Lil, her eyes wandering past Flynn's shoulder to take in the unfamiliar figure of Pablo.

Flynn, always quick on the uptake, saw the direction of her glance. He turned.

'Oh, this is Mr. Juarez, Lil. A man from Rio.'

Lil thrust out her hand. 'Pleased to meetcha, Mr. Juarez. I ain't heard a name like that before.'

41

The man from Rio clicked his heels together and bowing from the hips over Lil's hand murmured raptly: 'Charmed.' His lips rested for an instant on Lil's finger. His moustache brushed her skin like a butterfly's wing. It was a new sensation for Lil. And she was responsive to even the slightest sensations.

She laughed lightly.

'Hey, Gus! Take a look at this and learn something,' she cried. 'This man's had a bringin' up.'

'Pablo is my new assistant,' Rita said with open pride. Lil gave her a broad wink.

'Day or night work, Rita?'

Rita laughed.

'Both kinds,' she admitted frankly. 'Pablo is very much sought after by all the women in Rio.'

Lil's eyes swept over the gentleman in question.

'Yes, I should imagine,' she observed. She made a mental note to give him closer inspection at her leisure. She turned to Flynn, apparently dismissing Juarez from her mind. 'You're kind of a stranger, Flynn. Whose little shoes are under your bed now?'

'Nothin' like that, Lil,' Flynn assured her, enjoying her insinuation nevertheless. 'Since you come to town, I ain't had no hankerin' for what's around. I'm waitin' till I can have some luck like Gus.'

Lil gave him an arch glance. Flattery of any kind always delighted her. 'Well, Gus had his eyes open when I blew in. You want to keep awake, Flynn.'

'I'll do that little thing, Lil,' Flynn returned.

'Let's see your new pitchers, Lil,' Jordan suggested.

Lil was eager at once. She had brought them down with her in a large handbag. Now she drew out a number of 'cabinet' photographs, displaying her in a series of studied poses. Rita, Jordan and Flynn grouped around her. She held each print at arm's length for each to see. Skilfully, the photographer had included the whole of her diamond array in each picture, and she had brought to each pose the full value of her high-corseted breasts and swelling hips.

To one print she called attention as giving her style and dignity. Rita agreed with overflowing enthusiasm. Another pose displayed her hair, unbound, draped over a shoulder and spreading down to her tight waist.

'That's sorta simple and unaffected, don'tcha think?' Lil inquired.

There was a general murmur of approval.

'It make you look very virginal,' said Rita.

'God forbid!' retorted Lil, giving her a sharp look. Then she held up another photo with a pleased smile.

'Wait till you see this one. I show my legs in this.'

In this pose she stood over a chair with one knee crooked and resting on its seat. Her legs, sheathed in black, lace-clocked stockings, moulded the sensuous swell of her calves before disappearing discreetly under the hem of her gown.

'A little spicy, but not too raw,' she said, 'if you know what I mean.'

'Lemme look at that again, will you, Lil?' Flynn asked. 'Say, that's grand. You ain't got one to spare, have you? I mean, like this one.'

'You can have that one, Flynn, after I get through showin' it. It's for the bedroom. It'll keep you company when you're sleepin' alone.'

'You're a card, Lil,' Jordan said, with an uneasy laugh.

Lil now realized that Juarez hadn't seen the pictures. She looked around and saw that Pablo was leaning idly on his stick, watching her every move. She left the others and crossed to him.

'Want to see my pitchers?' Lil asked him. Her eyes widened and her voice took on a certain caressing warmth that sent a thrill down to Pablo's toes. He made a deep bow of assent.

Flynn, watching her, heard her query and caught her tone.

He frowned meditatively. Jordan called out to the bar for drinks.

Flynn turned to Rita.

'So you're stuck on this new Latin lover of yours, eh, Rita?'

'He is my own kind. He make love Latin way. That is hot like flame. We understand each other, Pablo and me.'

Dan Flynn still watched Lil, who was seated now, with Juarez bending over trying to get a look at her breasts as well as at her pictures. His expressive hands appeared to be illustrating his admiration for each picture as she held it out for him to examine.

Flynn turned to Rita with a smile that was part sneer. 'Better look out,' he warned, 'that Lil don't cop him away from you. He looks to me he's gone on her already.'

Rita's wide, full mouth curled scornfully. 'He hasn't enough money to tempt Lil. I see to that.'

Flynn laughed heartily. 'Keep 'im broke eh? That's a hot one.'

He strolled up to Lil and announced that he would be going along. Jordan swung back from the bar.

'All right, Flynn,' Lil said. 'Don't be a stranger.'

He shook hands with Juarez and promised that as soon as they could get together he would show Juarez the town. 'Gus is pretty busy, so I'll trot you around. Maybe we're not as interestin' as where you come from, but we got places, just the same. Well, so long, I got a date uptown. Up in the Flaming Twenties.'

Spider Kane joined him and they passed through the street doors. Lil frowned after them.

'God! A date up in the Twenties! I hope Flynn ain't hangin' out at Paresis Hall with the nances.'

'Nonsense, Lil,' Jordan exclaimed. 'Flynn likes skirts, not men. What would he be doing at Paresis Hall?'

'Well, I don't know.' Lil shook her head dubiously. 'A man that don't marry or keep a woman fer hisself just naturally

44

must be queer. If a man ain't got money to keep a girl regular, he'll at least pick up some chippies now an' then. An' Flynn's got money, but you don't never even see him with a dame. He's gotta have his satisfaction somehow. Now, don't he?'

Jordan would not be suspicious, even if he didn't like his rival. 'Maybe you're right about most men, but I'd never think that about Flynn. He's so big and masculine.'

Lil shot a quick, secret glance at the warm, dark, slender Juarez. 'Sometimes those big guys don't mean nothin' as lovers when you get to know them,' she said.

Jordan was a big man himself. He gave Lil a dark look. He was immediately pacified when she treated him to an engaging smile.

Outside, Flynn, with Spider Kane beside him, crossed the Square without speaking. When they turned into the Bowery he led Kane into a bar-room where they were the only patrons. 'I want to talk to Spider confidential,' he informed the bartender. 'Take a schooner on me and go drink it in a corner where you can't hear us.'

The bartender complied willingly. Flynn pulled at Spider's coat lapels, drawing him close.

'Now listen to this, Kane. I got the way to get the dope on Gus Jordan. It's all come to me. An' I'll get 'im right.'

Spider had to be convinced. 'I've heard you say that before, Boss. Gus is a hard guy to get.'

'An' I'm the bird that'll get him. Just because he stands in with the big mucky-mucks on Fourteenth Street ain't no reason why he can't be showed up same as anybody else, 'specially now that the reformers is stirrin' up hell. If I can get him, I'll be wearin' his shoes as the boss of this here district, and it'll be me who's the next sheriff.'

'That's all wool, Boss, an' a yard wide. But yer gotta have somethin' to go on.'

'I got it. Did you watch that greaser Rita brought up from South America?'

'Sure I watched 'im. He's better'n a blasted show, with that slobberin' over Lil's fingers like she was the guv'nor's dame.'

'All right. Lil ain't seen nothin' like him here in the States. An' if she falls for him he can get the whole drop on this girl game o' Jordan's. A woman will spill her guts to the man she's in love with.'

'A jane will do that sure,' Spider agreed promptly. 'But you're nuts if you think Lil knows anything about Jordan's business.'

'Nuts, am I? I know women, Kane. Lil ain't fell for Gus, has she? She's just usin' him. An' she had a good guy in Chi. Chick Clark, I've told you about. He was good in a different way from Gus. She didn't fall for him, did she? Crossed him pronto when she was done with 'im. She wants somethin' new. Somethin' different with new ideas about steamin' up a woman's blood. This feller's full o' ideas what's all new to Lil. An' I see she's gettin' herself ready to find out what those ideas is. That'd take the steam out of Gus.'

'Maybe so, Boss. Maybe so. Guess you can figger a woman to take her shirt off any time she shouldn't. But lemme tell you, Flynn. It'll be you monkeyin' with Diamond Lil; not me. I'd as soon take my dope dreams out of a pipe. I'm shovin' along. See you later.'

Kane pushed forward his brown derby and swung out of the place. Flynn looked after him for a moment and then grunted.

Ideas began to form in his mind. 'That greaser, Juarez, will do anything for money,' Flynn told himself. 'From what Rita says, she don't give him much. Maybe if I fixed him up so he could make a noise when he put his hands in his pockets he'd get me the dope I can take to the district attorney. Just lemme get the screws on Gus and Lil and his spot in this district'll be mine. Mine!' He grinned to himself at the thought. 'They'd be sayin, "Daniel J. Flynn for sheriff," and, "You now Diamond Lil? Well, she's Dan Flynn's woman."'

Flynn drew a deep breath. The thought of so much
almost within his grasp made him dizzy with ambition
grip tightened so on the glass in his hand that it br
spilling its contents along the top of the bar. He laugh
aloud and called out for another drink.

6

LIL GIVES A LESSON
IN PHILOSOPHY

WHEN Rita and Juarez had gone, promising to look in later that evening, Lil gathered up her photographs and prepared to go up to her room to rest a while and then dress for her entertainment at midnight.

Late afternoon drinkers were wandering in to moisten their throats after a day's work. Hustlers with early pick-ups began noisily to fill up the tables.

Gus stopped Lil at the foot of the stairs.

'Lil,' he began, 'I want you to do somethin' for me.'

'Yeah?' said Lil.

'There's a poor kid that drifted in here this afternoon, and she seems like in a bad way. She won't talk and she don't look the usual stuff around here. If she's straight and down on her luck I'd like to help her.'

'What do you want me to do?' Lil asked.

'Have a talk with her. Whatever's botherin' her, she'll spill it to you if you're sympathetic like.'

'All right. Send her up to the room. I'll try to get her story.'

'And listen, Lil,' said Jordan. 'If the kid wants to get away from New York, tell her we'll help her. I can fix up a trip for her with Rita. It won't cost her nothin'.'

In a few minutes after Lil had entered her room her door

opened ever so easily, and the timid woebegone little figure
of Sally slipped in. Lil turned and saw her, and almost at once
she realized that this girl was out of her element. She was by
this time hardened to pitiful sights, but the utter bewilderment and hopelessness of the creature before her touched a
chord of sympathy in Lil's heart.

But Lil did not like to think herself soft in any respect, so
that her attitude toward the girl, while friendly, was by no
means tender. She directed Sally to sit down.

The girl slumped on the edge of one of Lil's gold chairs.
Her empty blue eyes lifted now and again to sweep the
luxurious room blankly. When they came to the gold swan
bed they would drop, and the girl's shoulders would twitch.

Again, she would lift her glance to the woman who stood
before her mirror patting her hair, examining her diamonds
and spreading her photographs over the dresser. Lil watched
the girl covertly through her glass. She chose a moment
when Sally's eyes were downcast to walk over to her.

'Well, kid,' Lil started, 'let's have the long, sad story. If
you don't want to talk to Mr. Jordan, you can talk to me
confidential like. What you done? Committed murder?'

Sally shrank in her chair as if a blow threatened her. 'No,
no! Not that! I – never will, either.'

'Then the guy's alive, huh?'

The girl started, and looked up, wondering. 'How – how
did you know – there was a — ' A dry sob choked her and
she wilted into the chair again.

'There's always a man, ain't there? Come on, now, tell me.
What's the matter? You goin'ta have a kid?'

Sally's tears broke bounds. She buried her face in her
hands. Through her fingers her whisper rose brokenly: 'How
could you tell? I – told – nobody.'

'Why, it stands out all over you.' Lil's tone beat the girl
with derision at her making a tragedy out of such a simple
situation. 'What of it? It's being done every day, ain't it ?'

The flow of Sally's tears dried out. Lil saw that there were not many left to flow.

'When I went with him,' Sally whispered, struggling against the shock of memory and its disillusionment, 'he said we would be – married! I – I believed him.'

Lil smiled briefly. 'Sure you believed him. What 'n' hell would a woman do if she didn't believe a man? Go on sleepin' alone for ever, huh?'

Lil caught up a box of Sweet Caporal cigarettes from her bed-table. She was provoked by the silliness of the child's state of mind. Trouble over the lack of physical necessities she could understand. She'd been hungry herself, back in the first Chicago days. But Lil didn't believe in whining over a man, any man. There were plenty of 'em who would sleep with you when you wanted that service done. You could get that on any corner, and plenty of 'em ready to pay for the privilege. The only difference between them was that one was better company, or easier to put up with, or more profitable than another. And she could, when she was in good humour, sympathize with a girl who had been foolish and careless enough to let herself get caught with a baby.

But she had no understanding of a woman who got herself worked up over the man himself. Or over the baby itself. Good Lord!

She thrust the packet of cigarettes at the girl in the chair. 'Want a smoke?'

Sally drew away and shook her head. 'Oh no! I don't smoke cigarettes.'

Lil smiled tolerantly. She dropped the packet with an air of resignation, and sat down opposite the other.

'So you believed him, eh?' she said. 'Was you in the business?'

Sally looked at her, questioning. 'I don't know what you mean.'

'I see. Began your believin' on your parlour sofa in your

own home. That kinda business never brings you no place. Come on, now, tell me the rest of it. An' first, what's your right name?'

'It's Sally, like I said. Sally Glynn.' She poured out the whole story.

Lil nodded through a spiral of smoke. 'I know. An' you was so busy worshippin' 'im you didn't think about brats until you felt one comin' on an' then he took a one-way-ticket out the front door. Well, why don't you go home?'

Sally's protest brought her wildly to her feet. 'I can never go home! I'd be so ashamed – and – and father'd kill me.' She sank down with a moan, her whole body shaking.

Lil brought smelling-salts in a crystal bottle and held them under the girl's nostrils. 'Take a whiff of that.'

The girl obeyed her, shivered, and then made a brave effort to sit straight. She held her hands together so tightly that her nails cut little purple crescents in her palms.

'I want to die,' she said, with despairing calmness. 'A girl at the mission told me — '

Lil interrupted sharply. 'A skirt at the mission? You mean the Salvation Army?'

'Yes, ma'am. Down at Jacobsen's Hall. I went there last night because I was hungry and didn't have no place else to go. And this girl — '

Lil's interest had detoured into another channel. She snuffed out her cigarette end and again interrupted. 'Did you meet the captain?'

'Yes. The captain was very kind to me,' the girl said, her weariness repossessing her. 'He gave me supper and made me pray. He said prayin' would make things all right. But nothin' could make things all right.'

Lil nodded cynically. 'Swell chance them guys is got to pray brats away, ain't they? They can pray trouble outa your head, maybe, and they can pray you into a bed, but they can't pray a kid out of you. What's the main feller's name? The captain?'

'I heard he was Captain Cummings. After we'd prayed I felt like talkin' to somebody, an' I told him everything. He said he'd find my father and talk to him. Prayin' made me feel maybe everythin' would be all right, but this morning I knew I couldn't ever go home.' She battled her tears for a moment, gripped her hands again and went on in her hopeless monotone. 'I couldn't ever go home again. I sneaked out of the mission this morning while Captain Cummings was gone. He'll be – disappointed in me – and mad. But I wanted to die. A girl told me – Mr. Jordan's was a good place. But I ain't got no – poison, or anything.'

Lil's thoughts remained upon Captain Cummings.

'So you double-crossed the good-lookin' preacher, huh?' she said. 'Well, all you lost was a prayer and you got a friend instead. You gotta friend, hear me, that'll do more for you than him and his prayin'.'

Sally looked down, nodding her head slowly. 'Thank you, ma'am for bein' my friend. But there ain't nothin' you can do. I got to go to the river, I guess. An' I hate to – I hate to drown the – the little one.'

Lil got up and stood over her, resting a bediamonded hand upon a frail shoulder.

'You ain't goin' to drown nothin'. All you need is to get away some place. Change o' climate like.'

'Yes,' Sally whispered to a pattern in the bedroom rug. 'If I could only go 'way some place where no one would ever know.'

'Now you're talkin' with your head. How 'bout you goin' to South America, huh? How'd you like that?'

Sally started up, overwhelmed by sudden eagerness, as if hope had burst in the door to claim her. But hope quickly dissolved and she dropped back into her chair.

'South America!' Her voice was full of her hopeless marvel. 'That would be grand – so far away.'

'You want to go, then?' Lil asked, sharply.

Sally frowned, and stared at the 'friend' who surely would not torment her. 'How could I? I haven't any money – not even for poison.'

'A woman don't need no money if she's got any sense. And I don't mean that for a joke either.'

Hint of purpose in Lil's manner and tone, hint of meaning and, perhaps, even a plan, held the girl speechless. Hope seemed to creep in the door despite her reasoning that there never could be any hope at all. The woman who talked to her so friendly – so gloriously beautiful and substantial behind the blaze of her rich jewels – and with hair almost like her own, but more lovely, surely she was not being heartlessly cruel!

'Now lissen, kid,' Lil said, 'you'll understand my kind of language if you got any brains at all. You think you been handed a special smack on the chin 'cause you left the old folks an' home for the slicker who done you wrong. That story's been set to music long ago. You can get to South America all right. You admit that would help, don't you?'

'Oh – oh! If I only could!'

Lil spread her hands in a gesture that said eloquently that Sally's problem was that easily settled. 'You don't have to stay there, of course, if you don't want to. You can leave the son an' heir in the tropics, come back, and who'd be the wiser?'

Deep in Sally's blue eyes points of light began to crowd their emptiness. Cheeks that were alabaster white but a moment before were touched with colour. Her hands unfolded and caught the arms of Lil's gilt chair.

'I could – couldn't I? Nobody would know . . . ' Full flood of her eager dream bore her up from the chair, to stand her on her feet, and to press her hands against her throat under her cape. The lights in her eyes were like the sparks from Lil's pendants.

Lil smiled into her enthusiasm and rose to it heartily.

'Why, sure you could!' she agreed. 'Lots of other girls who

got into some guy's arms without crossin' their fingers has their kids down there. Flock of 'em every day.'

Sally hugged her dream as long as she could. Then her eyes slowly emptied.

'The first thing I'm goin' to do is dress you up, 'cause fine feathers make fine birds. Now, whadaya say, kid? Want to go?'

Blue eyes filled again and stared, pleading that belief would stay and not go away. Lil met their pleading with a steady gaze of her own. Sally caught her hand and wrapped her own quivering fingers about it, fingers that were warm and quick-pulsed at last.

Lil lit another cigarette. Sally watched her move across the room. Lil went into the hall and called downstairs. Bill heard her summons, and left his tray while he ran upstairs.

'Anybody in the music-hall?' Lil asked. 'Any of the janes, I mean.'

'Kitty's got a sucker with a white vest and a cane. She's gittin' him drunk. She's got all his small change now, an' she's worried 'bout a bill he's got in 'is wallet. It's a twenty an' she's afraid he'll remember it an' yap.'

'Tell Kitty I want her. She don't want the twenty anyhow, if it's all the guy's got left.'

'All right. I'll steer some other hooker on to him.'

She went back into the room and stood in front of the girl. 'Get yourself together and see yourself through,' she said.

Sally straightened, dabbed at her eyes, and set her lips firmly. 'I guess I'll have to. I – I guess he didn't love me, after all.'

'I suppose he was married?' she observed.

'Yes. But I didn't know – till afterwards. Honest, ma'am, I didn't.'

Lil reassured her with a languid wave of her hand. 'Makes no difference to me, kid, whether you did or not. I'm not like your Salvation captain who hands you prayers. Bein' married or bein' single don't make no difference in a man. He's only

54

got one game. What you got to do is to be smart enough to play the game their way. You'll learn.'

Kitty opened the door and came in. She looked curiously at Sally, and Lil gave her a hidden sign to guard herself.

'What do you want, Lil?' Kitty asked.

'I want you to buy this kid some clothes.'

Kitty waited while Lil fingered in the white box with the purple cover and brought out two or three bills. These she handed to Kitty.

'She needs a dress,' said Lil. 'Get her somethin' pretty, trimmed with lace. An' get her a hat, with a feather.' She turned to look at Sally's feet. 'How's your shoes, kid?'

Sally lifted her foot. Her tiny pointed shoes were shabby.

'Is everything you got on like them?' asked Lil. 'Worn out?'

Sally dropped her eyes shyly and nodded.

Lil gave Kitty the rest of her instructions.

'Get her some shoes and underwear. Here's another bill. An' since I'm givin' you the money, don't go tryin' to get nothin' for nothin'.'

Kitty took silent measure of the girl she was to outfit, counted the money Lil handed her, and went out. 'Sounds like you was gettin' a troosoo,' she said before she closed the door.

'You're awfully good,' said Sally to Lil. A flavour of worship crept into her tone.

'I'm glad I could do it for you, kid,' Lil returned.

Sally closed her eyes that she might vision herself in a new dress with lace. With a hat with a feather on it. And new shoes, and fresh white underclothes. She couldn't remember when she had been new all over. The gentleman downstairs and this golden-haired lady with so many diamonds must be awfully kind. There were good people in the world after all. She wondered if the prayers the good man at the mission had said with her had anything to do with it.

She was watching Lil with large round eyes. Lil was changing her dress. Sally thought she must be very, very rich. Her black stockings were silk, and when she stepped out of her petticoat Sally saw that clusters of diamonds nestled in the ribbon bows of her garters above her knees under the hem of a short chemise. The chemise was silk, also, and under it were edgings of real lace. She wanted to linger upon her, marvelling at such luxuriousness, but her thought was bothering her.

'How am I gonna get to South America?' she asked.

'Well, it's a cinch you can't swim,' said Lil without turning from her mirror. 'You have to go by boat.'

Lil turned to give the girl a comprehensive look. She nodded to her own thought, and said aloud, 'There'll be work for you to do, kid. You'll get along. So don't worry.'

'I don't know how I can ever thank you.'

Lil waved this dilemma aside airily. 'Who wants thanks for doin' a good turn? What'd you say your name was?'

'Sally. Sally Glynn.' Her voice trembled a little, and dropped when she spoke the name that swept her back to the home she had left, and to the arms from which she had been thrust.

'Tell you what you do,' Lil said. 'When you get down there change your name to Carmen.'

Jordan opened the door. He glanced at Sally, who got to her feet, fresh words of eager gratitude hovering on her quivering lips, but Lil pointed him back into the corridor. She went out with him and closed the door behind her.

'I couldn't have done it better if I'd had a Salvation Army bonnet,' she exulted. 'She's all set for an ocean voyage.'

'Charlie Fong's downstairs hanging 'round. He'll put her up at his place for the night.'

'You keep 'im waitin' a bit. Kitty's gettin' her some rags.'

Kitty came back with a silk taffeta that fascinated Sally with its rustle when she took it out of its box. Lil helped the girl strip to the skin. Sally was shyly bashful before the other's appraising gaze at her nudity.

'You'll be a hit in South America,' Lil remarked, while the white, fresh underthings were being slipped over Sally's head.

'I hope everybody likes me.'

'They will. They'll like you plenty.'

Lil took her down the back stairs and turned her over to Jordan. She was very pretty now, and proud of her new dress and hat and creaking shoes. She choked a little when she said to Gus:

'I'll never forget you, mister.'

Jordan looked at her with a new and quickly definite interest. Charlie Fong came close, smiling, his hands in his sleeves. Gus held him back with a gesture while he went on with his new thought. Suddenly he put the thought away with a shrug of resignation. There'd be complications if he kept the girl around any place. Lil had an uncanny way of tripping him up whenever he pulled anything on her.

'You go along with Charlie here,' he said. 'He'll take care of you until your boat leaves.'

Charlie bobbed his head and smiled into the girl's face, and she went out with him, through Jordan's side door into the dark alley that led through the back walls of buildings into Mott Street.

7

THE CHICKEN-COOP OF
CHARLIE FONG

CHINATOWN in New York was a transplantation of the Celestial Kingdom in many respects. That is, within the confines of Mott, Pell and Doyer Streets the saffron-faced Orientals had burrowed in, bringing with them not only the time-honoured customs of their Asiatic homes, but the virtues and vices of the yellow empire as well.

With becoming wisdom the little Orientals realized that, much as they tried to make themselves feel at home in this New World haven, yet they were in the midst of a white race with whom they must do business and depend upon for protection. And they understood, too, with that ageless resignation and practical calm which passes for Oriental wisdom, that they must submit to the terms of the white man, and that very often they must accept the blame and censure while the white man took the lion's share of the profit.

They felt the pressure of ward politics and they were forced to contribute generously to campaign chests and election expenses. They had their clubs and secret societies, the Hip Sing Tong and the On Leong Tong being the most powerful.

There were many honest and industrious Chinese in New York's Chinatown. Shopkeepers, merchants and importers of eminent respectability dwelt there honourably; men of the Mandarin class, who, when the business day was done sat in their houses and sipped their rice wine, while they discoursed to friends in the most cultured and learned fashion.

It was men of the coolie class, like Charlie Fong, shrewd, cunning, but completely without honour, who pandered to the white vice lords for pieces of silver. It was that type who dealt in white slavery, who maintained opium dens in the rookeries that bordered the alleys leading off Mott, Pell and Doyer Streets.

None knew better than Charlie Fong the devious passages of Chinatown, with their hidden traps – panels that slid noiselessly at the pressing of a spring and which closed as silently, shutting out the world like the door of the Death House at Sing Sing.

Charlie had that 'lean and hungry look', but his purse was well-lined with ill-gotten gains. His slant-eyed, muddy-yellow face had the sinister, cynical aspect of a fox's. When he smiled at you in what was supposed to be a friendly fashion you had the dreadful feeling that a snail was creeping up your spine. The long queue that hung down his back and was bound with a narrow red ribbon was often as expressive of emotion by its movement as his face.

He kept a store on Mott Street, ostensibly to sell Oriental knick-knacks and cheap curios to tourists and slumming parties. But his trade in that line was so small as to be negligible. It was just a front for his real trade. In the ramshackle frame building which by this time he owned there were two floors of rooms above the store. These rooms were hardly more than cubicles, drab, dim and dusty, furnished each with an iron bedstead, a battered chair and a wash-stand. The windows that fronted on the street were always closed by heavy wooden shutters, so that in summer the rooms were stifling. The rooms at the back, overlooking wash-lines of nondescript clothing, and backyards filled with all sorts of debris, had barred windows. In each room a gas-jet, when lighted, gave forth a sickly, funereal illumination.

When business was good Charlie Fong had one or two hopeful young things for each of his cubicles. But the most interesting part of Charlie's house was the cellar. This cellar, when you first descended into it, looked much like any other cellar. There was the usual accumulation of junk. Packing-cases in which Charlie had received his stock-in-trade; an assortment of empty tea-tins, empty rice-sacks, and a hundred and one other bits of rag-tag and bobtail. But at about the centre of the cellar under the cobwebby gas-jet was a large round rubbish-can with a cover.

If you lifted the cover you would see a pile of trash and would look no further. But if you had been present when Charlie lifted the cover you would have seen something quite different. Charlie would screw the cover around a few times, and when he lifted it off there would be a container attached to it. In the container would be the trash you had seen. Now if you looked into the rubbish-can you would see that it had no bottom and that you were looking into a black void out of which could be discerned the top end and rungs of a ladder. There was a sub-cellar.

The sub-cellar was nothing more than a hole in the ground about twelve by fourteen feet. The walls were of rough quartzite, and along three of them were bunks, with mildewed mattresses over which were thrown coarse horse-blankets. In the centre of the subterranean chamber was a low Chinese lacquer table with an opium smoker's layout upon it. In the centre of the little table was the lamp in the flame of which gum-opium was cooked on the end of a long needle for insertion in the bowl of a pipe.

The hard dirt floor, which was damp and sent forth an earthy odour to mingle with the ever-present fumes of past smokings, was covered with grass mats on which were painted Chinese ideographs in colours that were once bright but had long since grown mucky.

On the fourth wall hung a gong that looked like a brazen

moon, and beside it a mallet of ivory with a rounded head. Beneath these was a lacquer cabinet inlaid with mother-o'-pearl and embellished with carven dragons who stuck out their tongues. If you opened the doors of the cabinet you discovered that it had no back and that you were looking into the gloom of an underground passage.

But one other person besides Charlie Fong knew of the existence of that passage, and that was Gus Jordan. Even Chuck, who was Jordan's trusted lieutenant, and spoke Chinese like a native of Canton, was unaware of the tunnel which ended in the cellar of Suicide Hall.

Diamond Lil had long wondered how it was that Charlie would put in a sudden appearance at Jordan's; emerging from Gus's office after she had looked in to see if Gus was there and found the room empty. If she had examined the office carefully she would have discovered the trap-door that let Gus down into the cellar without anyone in the place knowing he was going there. Then, too, she had seen Gus go into his office and close the door, and when she went in to speak to him he was nowhere to be seen. It was rather amazing to her, and she had often promised herself to ask Gus about it. But she never got around to it, because above all she disliked argument, and intuition told her that somehow or other Gus would prove touchy on that point. She told herself, as long as he kept her supplied with the diamonds she loved, she didn't give a damn whether he was a magician or not. Lil was very superstitious, and she was not at all sure Gus wasn't practising black magic.

Charlie Fong had four girls at this time occupying the tiny rooms on his top floor. They had all answered the advertisement inserted in the morning papers. It was a standing advertisement paid for jointly by Gus and Rita. It sounded quite harmless. Witness:

WANTED – Pretty girls as entertainers, to dance and sing. No experience necessary. Must be willing to travel.

Easy work; good pay; pleasant environment. Unusual opportunity. Apply No. — Mott St.

When those who answered the advertisement found themselves greeted by a Chinese and invited to stay in his house they frequently went away. Others, not so squeamish, stayed, as Charlie in his pidgin-English explained that they could have free room and board until the great theatrical agent who was to give them their jobs arrived.

The addition of Sally Glynn, who was almost happy decked out in the finery Lil had purchased for her, brought the number of future whores up to five.

Charlie Fong was quite proud of his collection, and he awaited with eagerness the arrival of Gus and Rita. He longed to hear their commendations, and the rapturous murmurings of Rita as she gazed at each girl and envisioned her spread upon the bed of some Brazilian bordello. She always liked a fair sprinkling of blondes in the shipments, for the swarthy hombres of South America seemed to make a fetish of golden locks and bodies as white as new ivory.

Perhaps it was because they were jaded by the constant contact with the dark women of their race. The sight of light hair, light bodies amid the all-too-familiar brown, fanned the flame of their desires. It gave a fillip to their emotions, like the sight of a nude woman who has drawn on black silk stockings.

Gus Jordan had instructed Rita to meet him at Charlie's. He was rather anxious to get the whole business done. The truth was that Gus was becoming a little nervous about the nefarious game he was playing. The tip that he was being watched had him up in the air, because he didn't know who was doing the watching. You can't bribe a phantom. He wished in his heart that Rita had not come at this time, but as long as she had arrived he wished to God she'd clear out in short order. He wanted to get to Charlie's, rush though the whole business, no matter how many girls Charlie had on hand at the moment, and then pack Rita and the whole damn crew off to South America. More than anything else in the world, Gus wanted to be sheriff of New York County. It would not only give him prestige and put him in the political spotlight, but there would be plenty of easy pickings, and he could emblazon Diamond Lil with all the rocks she wanted and·make the good citizens fall down in adoration of her beauty and turn sick with envy of him.

As he prepared to enter his office and use the underground route that would swiftly take him to Charlie Fong's, Kitty came to him with the message that Lil wanted to see him in her boudoir.

Gus was nervously impatient to be off. He made a gesture of annoyance.

'What does she want, Kitty? Did she say?'

'Says she wants to talk to yer, Gus, that's all. Guess it's private witchou an' her.'

'All right, I'll go up.' He started towards the stairs leading to the balcony and Lil's room. He paused at the foot and turned to Kitty. 'Say, Kitty — '

'Yeah?'

'Wouldja be willin' to do me a little favour?'

'Sure, Gus. You know me. Anythin' at all for you or Lil. Why; if it wasn't for you an' her, I guess I'd — '

Gus smiled.

'Now cut that. Lissen, Kitty — ' He came close to her and lowered his voice. 'This is a chance to make a little money for yourself.'

Kitty's ears almost wiggled.

'I'm listenin',' she said eagerly.

Gus looked around and his lips came close to her left ear. 'Remember that guy McGee you used to pal around with?'

Kitty's face lit up, cracking its lacquer.

'Remember him! Jeeziz! How could I ever forget him? He had the biggest — '

'All right, all right,' Gus cut in. 'Now — '

'I was jus' gonna say that he had the biggest idea of hisself of any guy I ever met.'

'He's on the in with the bulls, ain't he?'

Kitty's lips curled derisively. 'He's a stoolie, if 'at's what yer mean.'

'Whatever he is, I don't give a damn. But he might be able to get some information for me. There'll be some coin in it for him, too, if he does.'

'I getcha.'

'Do you know where he is?'

'Yeah,' said Kitty. 'I never really los' complete trackt of him. I could always count on Spot for a t'rill when other geezers was like stale beer.'

'Good. See him as soon as you can and find out if he knows who's got me marked. If he don't, tell him to find out. And don't forget to say there's a slice of real mazuma in it for him.'

'I'm witcha, Gus. I'll do like you say. I'll getcha the dirt if I gotta go t'rough the police department to git it.'

'That's fine. Any time you need any help you can count on me.'

Gus found Lil recumbent upon her gold swan bed. She had just had a tubbing in perfumed water, and about her was a fragrant aura that made Gus think of summers he'd spent on a farm when he was a kid, with flowers growing all around and new-mown hay giving out a scent that made the heart beat quicker. He inhaled deeply, and his heart ticked rapidly as he viewed the gaudy Lil, who was yet lovely despite her gaudiness. Her peignoir was partly open and her fair breasts curved deliciously before his eyes.

'Want me, Lil?' he inquired somewhat huskily. He knew he would come whenever she called, and that always he would do her bidding even if it dragged him through hell.

Lil yawned charmingly behind a small hand. She smiled dazzlingly.

'You know I always want you, Gus,' she replied in answer to his question.

He drew near the bed. It would have been a natural thing for him to kiss her. But he did not. His mind was torn between her charms and his nervous desire to be about his business. He bit the end off a cigar, and when he held a flame to it his hand trembled slightly.

Lil's sharp, all-seeing eyes noticed it.

'What are you so nervous about, Gus? Anything gone wrong?'

Gus laughed self-consciously.

'I ain't nervous. What makes you think that? There ain't nothin' wrong.'

'Well, you act as if there was.'

'No, no. It's just that this is a busy day for me. I gotta appointment uptown on Fourteenth Street,' he lied. 'You know, a conference about the comin' election. If you ain't wantin' me for anythin' special, I better get goin'.'

Lil stretched out to the stand at the side of the bed and chose a cigarette. Gus fumbled for a match and lighted it for her.

'I been kinda thinkin', Gus, about that girl Sally.'

Gus stiffened.

'Now, forget about her, Lil. We done the best we could for her. An' that's that.'

'Charlie's puttin' her up over to his place, ain't he?'

'Y-yes,' Gus replied hesitatingly.

'Well, what kind of a joint has that Chink got?'

'Oh, it's a nice, clean, quiet place, Lil. She's in good hands there. Charlie's a gentle sort of a duck where women is concerned.'

Lil puckered her lips doubtfully.

'I ain't so sure about that. Personally, I don't think a tart'd be safe with that Chink. And you know that girl Sally ain't no tart, Gus.'

Gus knitted his brows impatiently.

'Well, what d'you want to do, Lil?'

Lil exhaled a long stream of cigarette smoke.

'I think it'd be better to let her stay in one of the rooms here till it's time for the boat to sail.'

'Hell, Lil, we can't have her moonin' around here. I'm tellin' you she's all right at Charlie's.'

'It's just a suggestion, Gus. You see, she's in the family way. Over two months gone now.'

Gus's brows shot upward.

'Jumpin' Jeeziz, Lil! Whyn't you tell me this before?'

Lil stared at him shrewdly.

'What the hell difference does it make whether you knew it or not?'

Gus reddened.

'Well, I mean — ' he stumbled. 'Hell, maybe we should've got a doctor for her or somethin'.'

'That's all very nice, Gus. But you didn't gimme a chance to finish what I was sayin'. The dame was over to the Salvation Army before she come here. They prayed over her an' give her a load of useless advice. But they keep check on the souls they're tryin' to save. Suppose they trail her here and find out we shipped her over to a Chink's joint? And her with a kid comin'. Why, it'd get out, and people'd say I ain't got no conscience. They'd say you an' me ain't Christian, Gus.'

'Aw, don't let that worry you, Lil.'

'It's the principle of the thing, Gus.' Lil flicked the ash deftly from the end of her cigarette. 'I thought Rita was goin' to get the kid out of the country right away. A week's gone by and she's still lingerin' around.'

'There ain't been a boat, Lil. There won't be none goin' down to Rio for another week or so.'

'Well, then, bring her over here till it's time for her to sail.'

Gus bit into his cigar and was silent for a moment.

'I'll tell you what, Lil. I'll talk to her. But if she's comfortable over to Charlie's, there ain't no sense in luggin' her in here and makin' extra work for people.'

Lil sniffed. 'If she's comfortable — '

'I gotta go, Lil. I'm late for that appointment now.'

'All right, Gus. See you later.'

Gus started to leave, but paused at the door.

'What are you goin' to do today, Lil?'

'I got a couple of things in mind.'

'Where you goin'?'

'Out.'

Gus stroked his beard.

'You ain't been seein' nothin' of this Jawrez, have you, Lil?'

'Who, me? Don't be silly. Whatsa matter? That twist Rita been puttin' ideas in your head?'

'No, but – you been goin' out quite a bit durin' the past week. You used to stick pretty close around here. Maybe I am too damn suspicious, Lil. But I can't help bein' jealous of you. You know I'd kill any guy that came between us.'

'Aw, now listen, Gus. Don't go lettin' your imagination paint vile pitchers of me. It ain't right.'

'I'm sorry, Lil. Well, so long. Be back in a couple of hours.'

'So long, Gus. And don't forget about seein' that dame Sally.'

'I won't, Lil. I sure won't.'

Gus closed the door after him and drew a deep breath.

He made all possible speed in getting over to Charlie's. He was worried by Lil's renewed interest in the welfare of the tragic Sally. If he'd known the girl was pregnant he would not have figured on her as another item in the shipment down to Rio. Well, he told himself, let them find out about it after she'd arrived in Brazil and been paid for. He wasn't going to worry about it. But as far as bringing Sally to his

67

place till the boat sailed – that was definitely out, whatever Lil had to say about it. It was too damn dangerous.

He made his way up from Charlie's cellar to the room behind Charlie's store, where he found both the Chinese and Rita waiting for him.

'What ees the matter weeth you, Gus?' Rita cried. 'We wait and wait and you not come. So much time ees waste.'

'Shut up, Rita!' Jordan barked. He was in a bad temper. 'Hey you, Charlie. Get a whisk-broom and brush me off. How many times have I told you to keep that infernal pas — ' He caught himself and looked at Rita. 'That blasted alley is full of dirt. Look at me!'

Charlie began whisking him off.

'How many are there?' Gus demanded of Fong.

'Five alla 'gether,' said the Chinese. 'Velly plitty. Nice, nice!'

'Five!' Jordan snorted. 'That's countin' the one you brought over from my place, eh? What's the matter? Ain't that advertisement bringin' a better response than that?'

Charlie Fong bobbed his head and his queue flew back and forth. 'Many many come. Many go way. No wantee job. Allee same flighten likee litty bird.'

'This ees ver' bad, Jordan,' Rita remarked. 'We mus' wait for more. Eet does not pay to take less than ten girls.'

'Damn' nuisance!' Jordan snapped. 'I'd hoped you'd be on your way in a few days. I don't like the idea of keepin' this Sally dame around too long. She's been to the Salvation Army and they might get nosey about her.'

Rita shrugged. 'They weel not theenk to look here at Charlie's. Remember, she is not bad-looking. She weel bring beeg money!'

'Yeah,' Gus agreed grudgingly. 'But she may prove more trouble than she's worth.'

Rita tapped her breast. 'You leave ever'thing to me, Gus.'

'All right. Whatever you say. Only my hands are clean, see.'

Rita smiled caustically. 'Of course, Gus. I am the only one whose hands are soiled, eh?'

'That's up to you,' Gus snarled. 'Well, let's get going. Drag out the girls, Fong, and let's look at 'em. I gotta get back.'

'Oh, no doubt Lil ees waiting impatiently, eh?'

'What's it to you if she is? Cut it, and get down to business.'

'You are in one awful bad temper, Gus.'

'Charlie, let's go up in that parlour of yours. Can't tell who might wander in here.'

Charlie led them up to the next floor and showed them into a room furnished in what Fong considered the height of Oriental luxury. It gave forth the odour of incense. To Gus it smelt like hell and he said so. Charlie merely grinned.

Gus dropped his bulk on to a divan and masticated the end of his cigar. Rita fluttered about, while Charlie darted out of the room to rustle up the girls.

Gus suddenly bounced up and started after Charlie.

'Hey! Wait! Don't bring in that Sally. She's all right. Let's see the rest.'

Charlie Fong nodded and padded up to the top floor in his felt slippers.

Gus returned to the parlour and once more flopped on the divan.

'How's your friend Jawrez, Rita?' Gus inquired casually, although his eyes were fixed on her.

'Pretty good, Gus.'

'Behavin' himself, Rita? You know this town is full of women ready to pick up a slick article like him.'

Rita raised her chin. 'Pablo knows better than to misbehave. I have got him trained, Gus.'

'What's he doin' with himself? I ain't seen him around much except a couple of evenin's at my place with you.'

'Meester Flynn is showing him the town.'

'Flynn, eh? Well, now, that's nice. Him and Dan Flynn

ought to get along great together. Flynn has a way with him.'
His eyes narrowed but did not leave Rita's face.

She smiled. 'You do not like Flynn, Gus?'

Gus rolled the cigar about in his mouth before he replied.
'Oh, Dan's all right. I've known him since I was a boy. He's
inclined to be ambitious, Rita. He'd like to get on top, but
he ain't willin' to work hard to get there.'

'I see. Perhaps, he – er – how you say? – expects to get
there by his wits.'

'Oh, Flynn's got brains all right. He's pretty smooth. But
it takes more than brains if you want to get anywhere in
politics. You got to do a lot of favours and you got to have a
personality that people take to. Now, Flynn — '

But Charlie was in the doorway ushering in four girls, who
giggled and seemed not to know what to do with their hands.

'Well, well, well,' said Gus, rising with a broad smile.
'Come in, girls. Don't be bashful.'

'My!' exclaimed Rita. 'What pretty, pretty girls!'

8

LIL STARTS SOMETHING

GIRLS who responded to the advertisement and then were willing to put themselves under Fong's wing, so to speak, till they could be inspected by the 'theatrical agent' were of a type that had no important home ties. Many of them had a certain amount of talent in the way of dancing and singing, or thought they had, and it was seldom that there was a virgin in the group. At the same time, none of them was particularly worldly-wise, although some of them liked to think they were.

Each had a story behind her, but it was the story of the hundreds, the thousands. It was the story of a little ambition and a great hope; of immense trust and a few brains; of false pride and tragic courage. They were but units in the great mass of humanity which seem destined to struggle vainly for any realization of happiness and who go under in the backwash of the tide of living.

These girls that Charlie Fong presented to the scrutiny of the discriminating Rita were of that character. Their names, she learned, were Violet, Bessie, Polly and Adelaide.

Violet was small, raven-haired, with firm, cup-like breasts. Under dark hair and eyes her skin was very pale. Her mouth was red and full-blooded. She looked as though she and passion were far from strangers. Rita was quite satisfied with her.

Bessie had gentian-coloured eyes set in a heart-shaped face. She was rather tall, with large, full breasts. She was a bit thick through the hips, Rita noted, but South American Lotharios were not averse to pillow-like buttocks. Yes, Bessie was marketable.

Polly was plump, but delightfully formed. To use a term of the Ghetto, she was *zaftig*. Great plaits of auburn hair were coiled about her head. Rita could tell from looking in the girl's eyes that she would be docile. She would sell for a pretty penny.

The girl Adelaide had more poise than the others. Rita sensed at once that she had been around more. There was a tightness about her lips that informed the experienced Rita that Adelaide would not be so easy when she woke up to what she was going into. Her hair was just a shade off blonde. She was of the attractive Scandinavian type, with something of that race's flair for adventure, yet having also its reserve and self-containment. Rita figured the girl might be troublesome, but then, a little bleach on that hair so already near the desirable blonde, would make her very valuable. Money was money, and girls were girls. She knew that Jordan, especially after his talk with her a while previous, would be angry if she turned the girl down.

She beamed upon the four girls and her voice was gentle; her words were as honey.

'Lovely!' she exclaimed. 'You are all such lovely girls.' She shook a finger at them playfully. 'You are all good girls, eh? Not bad? No bad habits?'

The girls looked at one another and giggled.

'Oh yes, ma'am,' said Bessie. 'We're good girls. I am, anyhow.'

The others, with the exception of Adelaide, laughed at the smug avowal, and gave Rita knowing glances.

'I am delighted with all of you,' Rita announced effusively. 'Now, let me see your legs.'

'Say, we're goin' down to South America to sing, ain't we?' Adelaide asked slowly.

'To sing and dance, if necessary,' Rita replied. 'Come, show me your legs. I must see them.'

'Well, I tell you, lady,' Violet put in, 'if I depended on my legs for a living I'd starve to death.' She raised her skirts ever so little, disclosing legs that were slender, but well-formed, nevertheless.

The other girls followed suit, raising their voluminous skirts and petticoats, but none higher than the swell of their calves. Adelaide showed only a few inches above her ankles.

They dropped their dresses quickly when they became conscious of Jordan's scrutiny.

'I am satisfy,' said Rita. 'I wish only to see that you have not what you call the bow-legs.'

'Them South American men likes to look at legs,' said Polly wisely.

'Do we have to wear short dresses like they do in the music-halls?' Violet wanted to know.

'Oh, you weel have ever'thing of the best. Do not worry,' Rita said convincingly.

'Look here, lady,' said Adelaide. 'I only sing American songs. Do you think they'll understand me?'

'Music is a universal language, is it not?' Rita declared with an airy wave of her hand. 'It ees like love.'

The girls giggled at that.

'How much do we get paid?' Adelaide inquired shrewdly.

Rita shot an uncertain glance at Jordan. He caught it.

'I tell you girls,' he said, addressing them for the first time since they had entered the room, 'the sky's the limit as to what you can earn. It all depends on your – er – talent, and ability to please the people down there. But you'll all get along. You're smart girls, I could see that as soon as you come in.'

Even the cautious Adelaide was satisfied by that pro-
nouncement, since Jordan had an easy air of importance and
his words had the ring of sincerity.

'Yes, yes,' Rita went on hurriedly. 'You weel make plenty of
money. Theese ees one gran' opportunity. Eet comes but
once in a lifetime.'

'When do we sail, lady?' Bessie asked eagerly.

'Just a few days more, girls,' Jordan answered for Rita.
'There are a couple more girls going with you. We gotta wait
till they arrive. You'll have a lot of fun. It'll be like one big
family. It's a great trip. I wish I could take the time to make
a trip like that myself. But I'm too busy a man.'

Violet, whose mind ran to clothes more than the others,
piped up:

'What kind of stockings must we wear? I heard them
Spanish dames wears lace round their legs you can see the
skin through.'

For answer, Rita raised her own skirt that the girls might
see her stockings; smooth silk sheaths. 'You wear like I wear,'
she said.

'Ooh!' cried Polly. 'Silk stockin's! Won't that be grand,
girls?'

They echoed her glee with squeals of delight.

Jordan looked at his huge watch and then turned to the girls.
'You run along now, girls. Charlie, take good care of them. See
that they get plenty to eat. Fix 'em up somethin' special.'

Charlie bobbed in assent.

'Oh, thank you, mister,' the girls chorused, and, giggling
and prattling among themselves, they were shooed out by
Charlie. The Chinese returned almost at once.

'How's that Sally dame you got over at my place, Charlie?'
Jordan demanded. 'She behavin'? Seem contented?'

Charlie nodded furiously. 'Yiss, yiss. She velly glood one.
I catchee nicee room alla floor by self. Allee daytime she
puttee on tlakee off new dless. I watchee allee same keyhole.

Plitty blody. Plitty blody. She make lolla money when men see nakee.'

Lil dressed leisurely when Gus had departed to keep the appointment he told her he had with the big-wigs on Fourteenth Street. Even if she had known he was lying when he told her that, she would have said nothing, but she would have been suspicious and found some way of verifying her suspicions without letting Gus know.

She was perfectly indifferent as to how Jordan made his money, as long as he did make it, but she would have drawn the line at white slavery had she known that that traffic was his chief source of revenue. Lil was funny that way. Certainly sex held no mysteries for her. But if she knew that most of the money that Gus spent to buy her diamonds came from the marketing of women's bodies she would have resented it strongly. True enough, she had sold her own body, but she had always been complete mistress of herself and her emotions; she had never been a pawn in a man's game. These girls who were rustled down to Rio were no better than sheep led to the slaughter. They had not her strength of mind, her ability to make cool decisions, not her all-alluring voluptuousness that bent men to her will. She felt an instinctive sorrow for women who lacked her capacity to keep the predatory male under control.

Perhaps Gus sensed something of the sort in Lil, else he must have whispered a great many of his secrets to her when under the spell of her caresses.

· Twice during the past week, when Lil had been out driving in her hansom, she had encountered unlooked-for incidents. The first one occurred while old Mike was driving her near Castle Garden. Lil frequently chose that spot, where she could look out over the river where it merged with the Bay, and, too, she liked to study the colourful bits of humanity that passed through Castle Garden to a new existence for better or worse in the New World.

She was sitting in her carriage much amused by the apparent bewilderment of a group of immigrants that had just been freed by the Customs. They chattered like monkeys in their native tongue, which happened to be Rumanian but to Lil it was just a jargon of discordant sounds. They were very picturesque. The men as well as the women all neatly starched and stiff with bursts of colour in scarves, kerchiefs and shawls. Red, yellow, and blue. They had such a lost look, and they frequently peered here and there at the ground, as though they had dropped something, or, rather, expected to find something. Indeed, they had heard that the streets of the New World were paved with gold, and they were mystified and disappointed that so far they had not seen anything that remotely resembled the precious metal.

Lil was engrossed in their antics when a voice spoke very close to her left ear. She turned her head to find Pablo Juarez leaning into the cab.

'Good day, beautiful lady,' Juarez said, accompanying his words with a flash of white even teeth. 'I am indeed fortunate to find you alone. Always you have so *many* around you.'

Lil smiled back. 'I'm glad to see you, Mr. Juarez.' She extended her hand.

Juarez received it firmly in his and bent over it. 'Permit me.' His lips brushed her fingers.

'Come on in. There's plenty of room,' Lil invited.

Juarez got into the hansom with alacrity. Lil shut the trap in the top of the cab, which gave them privacy from the eyes and ears of Mike. But Mike was dozing, anyway, so it wouldn't have mattered.

'What are you doin' around here?' she inquired, at the same time taking note of the South American's perfect grooming. 'Got some relatives comin' in?'

'Oh no, no,' said Juarez. 'I am jus' seeing your so wonderful city. Mr. Flynn has been so good as to show me things. But today, I say to myself, 'Pablo, you will go alone into the great city and seek adventure.'

'Hmm. That's interestin'.' Lil remarked. 'Found any?'

'I have found you.'

Lil laughed.

'I didn't know I come under the head of adventure. Still, one never knows. Can I drive you anywhere, Mr. Juarez?'

'Please to call me Pablo. I would be so glad. Everybody call you Diamond Lil. I should like to be as informal. Weeth you above all, my dear lady.'

Lil gave him that certain look.

'Well, I ain't no criterion of convention myself, God knows. So, Pablo, if you're headin' some place I'll be glad to drop you off there.'

'I theenk I shall go to the Hoffman House Bar. But please to drive slowly. I treasure these moments weeth you, believe me.'

'You certainly 'got a way of puttin' things.' She pushed open the trap. 'Hey, Mike, brush them flies off of you and let's get goin'.'

Mike sat up with a jerk.

'All right, ma'am. All right. Where did ye say?'

'I didn't say. But you can drive us over to the Hoffman House, and don't be more'n a week gettin' there.'

Mike's weak eyes stared down through the trap and saw Juarez's top-hat. 'Lord ha' mercy!' said Mike.

Lil for several days imagined that her meeting with Juarez had been purely an accident. She found the Brazilian to have a charm that was new to her. Nevertheless, she was not more than normally interested in Juarez. He was Rita's man. The woman had made that clear, and Lil was never inclined to run after any man. She had never done so. Men had always sought her out, and she had always been in a position to choose from them to her best advantage. She liked Gus, although she did not feel that deep affection for him which is usually labelled love. He was good to her, satisfied her every whim, so Lil saw no reason, nor felt any desire, to make a change in the way of a man.

Lil had never been really in love. The genuine article hadn't come to sweep her heart beyond the government of her brain. Perhaps if some man came along who could give her bigger and better diamonds than Gus, she might be willing to change her address and her bed. Until then, she was satisfied to remain where she was. Much as Lil enjoyed sensual pleasures, her sexual passion was not as strong as her passion for diamonds.

There came a second meeting with Juarez while she was out driving. This was also accidental as far as Lil was concerned, but she began to think that it was less of an accident on Juarez's part.

She had been to get a fitting of a new gown she was having made. It was a beautiful affair of Chinese red that would go marvellously with her blonde hair when entertaining midnight slumming parties in Gus's dance-hall.

When she came out of the dressmaker's she found Juarez standing by her carriage. He gave her a hand and assisted her in.

'I recognize your carriage an' coachman,' he told her by way of explanation. 'I thought I wait.'

'Oh, you did,' Lil returned. 'Guess I can't stop you from that. If you're goin' my way, climb in.'

When he was seated by her, she said:

'Sure this is just an accident, you bein' here? You ain't been followin' me, have you?'

Juarez smiled, and raising her hand kissed it. 'Believe me, I would follow you to the end of the earth.'

'I ain't goin' that far,' she retorted with a laugh. 'You'll be savin' yourself a lot of trouble if you drop in at the place when you want to see me.'

'Bah! When I go to Jordan's, Rita ees always stick to me

like one leech. Then there ees Jordan around, and this one an' that one. I never see you alone.'

'Well that's true,' said Lil. 'But, you see, I'm kind of a public figger. People come special to Gus's to see me. My time ain't always my own.'

'That ees exactly why I follow you when you go out.'

Lil flashed him a look beneath her lids.

'Oh, so you have been followin' me. It ain't just an accident that you met me by Castle Garden, and here today? I was beginnin' to think there was somethin' funny the way you turned up out of nowhere.'

She was a little annoyed, yet to a certain extent flattered that the handsome Juarez should run after her. But then again she held a slight feeling of contempt for men who ran after her, unless they had money. She knew Juarez hadn't any.

Juarez still held her hand, his eyes fixed on the huge solitaire that Gus had but recently given her. She saw his look.

'Like it?' she asked.

'It ees beautiful. It must be ver' valuable.'

'All my rocks is valuable,' Lil reminded him. 'I don't go in for no junk.'

'I would like to give you all the diamonds in the world,' said Juarez ardently.

Lil gave him a quick glance.

Juarez shrugged his shoulders.

'Alas! I am too poor.'

Lil smiled secretly. 'Well, we can't have everythin'.'

'That ees only too true,' he said sadly. He clasped her hand passionately. 'If I was rich you would have me, no? You would smile upon poor Pablo, you would not be cold to him, you would — '

'Don't let your imagination get the best of you,' Lil interrupted. She knew now that Juarez was hopelessly head over heels in love with her. She saw at once that he would furnish a certain amount of amusement for her, without putting her in a difficult situation. She was intrigued by his personality, but she experienced no emotion as yet that would lead her into deep water with him. She could handle him to her own satisfaction.

She gave him no encouragement, but she liked his company and the homage he paid her. She knew, of course, that a word would bring his arms around her in a wild, passionate embrace. That knowledge gave her a sense of power, and she enjoyed it to the full.

However, today Jordan's question as to whether she had been seeing Juarez gave her something to think about. Had someone seen them together, or had Gus just tried a shot in the dark because he was jealous of any man who so much as looked at her with anything approaching a longing glance?

She knew that today, when she went out, Juarez would manage to meet her as he had done before. But she decided that she must warn him that they were being suspected of meeting, and that thereafter he must see her only at Gus's place. She did not relish crossing Gus now, when he was headed upward politically.

As she had expected, after Mike had driven her out of the neighbourhood of Suicide Hall, Juarez put in a sudden appearance. He got into the hansom quickly.

'Oh, I am so happy to see you!' he cried. 'Every day I watch and you do not come. I theenk you are mad with me. Today you come. I am overjoy'.'

'Wait a minute,' Lil said. 'Somebody must've seen you followin' me around. I can't get into no trouble with Gus, you know. You better not meet me like this no more. You'll have to come to the place if you want to see me.'

Juarez's mouth fell open. His face was a picture of despair.

'Not see you alone again!' he exclaimed miserably 'It ees a knife you stick in me. I would rather die a thousand deaths than this. Believe me, I adore you. I am yours, soul and body. Do not send me away, I beg, I implore you.'

Lil looked at him for a full minute without speaking. His face, so close to hers, was even more handsome in its sorrow. The hands that clasped hers trembled. The eyes that pleaded with her burned with an adoration she had never read in any man's eyes before. No, not even in the eyes of Chick Clark, who had loved her madly.

Her gaze swept over him. Her eyes narrowed. She pushed open the trap and called to Mike.

'Drive us over to Elizabeth Street, Mike. I'll tell you where to stop.'

'Where are we going?' Juarez asked in a hoarse whisper.

'We've got to go some place where we won't be seen,' she said slowly.

Juarez gasped, and then perspiration broke out on his brow. His tongue clove to the roof of his mouth. He could say nothing.

As the cab turned into Grand Street on its way to Elizabeth Street, Dan Flynn pushed through the doors of a corner saloon and saw them.

The cigar fell from his mouth and hit the ground. He pushed his derby to the back of his head. Then his mouth widened into a broad grin.

'Well, I'll be a son of a bitch!' he exploded.

9

TOUCH AND GO

L IL was made uneasy by Juarez's impetuous advances in the cab. She saw plainly enough that he was burning with a passion almost beyond his control, and she did not want him to explode in the public highway.

She knew he was desperately in love with her. She had seen the beginnings of it when in the first few nights after his arrival he had sat among the tables at Gus's with Rita. In the way he looked at her while she was entertaining the late crowds she had seen that his eyes followed her every move with rapt attention and something of desire.

The manner in which he had followed her during the past week, and now his open proclamations of adoration, left no room for doubt as to the height of which his desire for her had mounted.

He did interest her even at the first meeting with him. His polish, his refinement, combined with the knowledge that he was the most distinguished toreador in Rio, alone led her to speculate upon his abilities as a lover. A champion in the bull arena, she wondered if he could conduct himself equally well within more limited confines. It was only for the reason that she did not wish to chance any trouble with Gus that she had kept Juarez at a distance this long.

Today, the fierce protestations of love that Pablo Juarez

poured out to her, and his anguish when she appeared to be sending him away from her, struck a responsive fire within her. She came to the abrupt conclusion that now or never was the golden opportunity to test the quality of a Spaniard's love.

She had been faithful to Gus since she had taken up with him. But Lil believed in destiny. She felt that if it was not so intended, Fate would not have thrown Juarez into her path, particularly at a time when Gus's brand of loving had begun to pall. And who was Lil to go against the dictates of destiny?

The powerful Gus Jordan was a good man physically, but he lacked finesse. To Lil, love was as much a fine art as sculpture or music and the body was a sensitive instrument that rendered wonderful symphonies of exquisite rapture when played upon by a master of sexual counterpoint. Gus was as one who picks out a melody with an uncertain finger.

Chick Clark had been really quite remarkable as a lover. Lil often thought about him. What Chick had lacked in technique he had made up for by imagination. And he had really loved her with every fibre of his body and soul.

These thoughts occurred to Lil before she instructed Mike to drive them to Elizabeth Street. She asked herself what possible harm there could be in making the love-sick Juarez happy for a brief hour or two. She told herself that she had nothing to lose morally, and physically – well, you never missed a slice off a cut loaf. And besides, she would learn to her satisfaction and perhaps great pleasure, once and for all, whether or not these Spanish guys were really the lovers they were cracked up to be, or if their reputations were just founded on the hot dreams of silly virgins who read mushy novels. Lil liked to keep straight on her geography.

It was thus Lil thought of the quiet seclusion of Frances's room for her experiment. She did not know, of course, that Dan Flynn had seen her and Juarez together, else she would have hesitated about going through with her plan.

Leaving Mike and the cab at the corner, she and Juarez walked to the building wherein Frances maintained a room for such purposes as pleased her fancy at any given moment. Frances was one of the better-known girls at Gus's with whom Lil was friendly; whom she had, in fact, taught to be one of the best shoplifters in the business.

The room was over a wine-shop, and although Lil expected Frances would be out, she knew that the janitor was a frequenter of Jordan's and would let her into the room.

They located the janitor, and he came up from his hole in the basement. Richer by a coin Lil passed to him, he wiped the tobacco-juice from the corner of his mouth with the back of his hand and agreed to let them in.

They followed him into the hall, which was dark and smelt of wine-dregs from the shop on the first floor. The janitor stood aside to let Lil pass, but she instructed him to show the way.

He mounted the stairs, Lil followed, and Juarez brought up the rear. He was biting his lower lip till it almost bled. Inside of him was a raging volcano of tempestuous desire. The swaying movement of Lil's well-turned hips and the rhythm of her thighs ascending the stairs on a level with his eyes almost drove him mad. It was all he could do to beat down the terrific temptation to seize her then and there and disclose all her charms to his longing eyes. The rustle of Lil's taffeta skirt, the divine fragrance of the scent she was wearing, together with an odour of warm, pulsating flesh, had Juarez in a frenzy.

Suddenly the janitor had unlocked a door and was showing them into a room, which was bright with sunshine streaming through the window that looked out upon the street.

The janitor went out. Lil stepped at once to the window and drew the shade. Before she could even turn round she felt herself in Juarez's arms. He held her in a fierce, vice-like embrace and his hot lips were pressed to the nape of her neck. She turned as his arms relaxed their tension and met his lips with her own warm, sensuous ones.

Gus Jordan became a pale ghost in the back of Lil's mind. The present moment was an all-consuming flame. She felt herself swept from her feet, and presently the world became a place of exploding stars and bursting suns. Every nerve throbbed with a pleasure that was a refinement of pain. And then suddenly the soul hung suspended in sublimity.

And then – back to earth. The walls, the windows, the chairs, the bed, returned to entity.

Juarez could hardly believe his good fortune. Diamond Lil, the beautiful, the much-sought-after, had been his. And there she lay, watching him through slumbrous lids, a half-smile lazily curving her lovely lips.

Lil, on her part, was thinking that the youngest toreador in Rio was more than a champion. He was an artist, and she regretted that she had waited this long to find it out.

This more or less swift and impromptu affair merely whetted her sensual appetite.

Juarez seized her hand and rained kisses upon it.

'My adorable one! My beautiful! I am mad weeth happiness! You have been generous! You have been excr-r-ruciatingly kind to Pablo! Believe me, you have given me all that I would gladly die for. Nevair have I known a woman like you! Nevair have I known such love! You are marvellous! You are wonderful! You are divine!'

'You're not so bad yourself.' Lil smiled at him.

'Then you like me? You are not mad weeth me?' he cried 'I have made you to understand how much it is I love you?'

'Well, you've made me understand you've got a brand of lovin' that's in a class by itself,' Lil assured him. 'You never learned that in no bull arena.'

Juarez clasped his hands together joyously and his teeth glistened in a happy smile.

'Eet ees nothing to how Pablo shall love you, my beautiful!

I swear I shall make you gloriously happy. I shall die to make you happy!'

'You won't be no use to me dead.' Her eyes swept him from head to foot. 'God, you're strong. But you don't look it in them clothes.'

Pablo sprang up and moved his arms. 'I am like the iron underneath. Feel!' He extended an arm for her to feel the muscle.

Lil tested it with her fingers.

'Yeah! You're built for speed an' endurance like a greyhound.'

He looked down at the bulge of her breasts beneath her corset.

'Eet ees a crime that so beautiful a body as yours should be hidden away in so much clothes. I see you in your picture over the bar, and my heart turn over weeth admiration and envy that you are not mine. Since first I see you so, I have dreamed of you ever' night. Ever' night I dream that I hold your so white, so beautiful body in my arms, an' am so happy I know not what to do.'

Lil laughed.

'Catch you with a body in your arms an' not knowin' what to do.'

'But I speak true, my lovely one. I dream of you so, an' I am crazy weeth happiness. Then, alas! I wake up an' eet ees only a dream, an I am so miserable. I pray, I pray for my dream to come true.'

'You should've prayed to the devil. That's a hell of a favour to be askin'! Even I know that much.'

'I would give my chance of heaven for that dream to come true. To hold you in my arms, like I see you in your picture.'

'Well, here goes your chance of heaven!' cried Lil, with a laugh of abandonment.

Deftly she began to perform some operations that held Juarez spellbound.

He threw up his hands. '*Sacrè!* Can this be true? Do I still dream?'

'Can't you tell?' she retorted.

She dropped the last garment to the floor and her white body rose up from her clothes like Venus from her sea-shell.

Juarez was held breathless in amazement for the space of a few seconds, but he was equal to the situation.

It became a mad hour stolen from eternity. A mad hour in which every minute ran by with an exquisite, rapturous ache in its dying heart. Reason was nowhere, time was an immovable object nailed high on the wall, except where the world kept shop. To the lovers, only the senses were living, and beyond them was only a void in which the shriek of the city was but a faint voice crying itself to sleepy silence.

Who can say that in that one wrung hour they had not lived a thousand years of emotion?

'Honey,' Lil said, after a while, 'you're good. I often thought about you Spanish guys. I ain't a bit disappointed.'

'And you are more than I ever hoped to expect,' Juarez said fervently.

Lil didn't doubt that. Chick Clark always said that if she ever stayed with a king for a night he'd give her the queen's jewels next morning.

'Then you like me better than your Spanish women?' she asked, stretching her body languidly.

'Ah!' he exclaimed. 'Beside you, my beautiful, they make love like a child. You are eeneemitable!'

'I'm what?' she inquired. Lil often sprung an unexpected word herself, and with devastating effect. But the Brazilian's foreign pronunciation baffled her.

'Eeneemitable! No one can equal you. No one can eemeetate you!'

'Oh, I'm inimitable! I gotta remember that. Gus oughter known about me bein' inimitable. Lemme see, when I come downstairs tonight he can announce 'the one and only – the inimitable Diamond Lil.' That oughter tear 'em up!'

Juarez clutched her hand. His glance rested once more, as it had done divers times, upon the huge solitaire on her finger.

'I 'ave nevair seen a stone of such a size,' he murmured.

'I got that for havin' bedroom eyes!' she laughed.

He smiled at her 'I cannot credit my good fortune, that I am here weeth you!'

'You knew what I was bringin' you up here for, didn't cha?'

'I but scarcely dared to hope! When did you decide that you would have me, my gracious one?'

'Well, when I first saw you, I says to myself: "Some afternoon when I ain't got much to do I'm gonna have that."'

'What kind of men ees it you like?' he asked.

'Well, I'll tell you. A lot depends on my mood. But as a gen'ral thing, I likes a guy that's a gentleman in public but a bum in a bedroom. That's a kinder broad statement, but you get the idea.'

Her eyes drifted over to the dial of Frances's alarm clock, which stood on the dresser. The afternoon was more than half over. Juarez saw the direction of her look.

'Do not theenk of going yet, I beg of you!'

'Don't worry. With a guy I likes I gen'lly takes my time. You can turn back the clock, honey.'

'You are adorable!'

'Say, you ain't by any chance tellin' me the same stuff you tell to Rita?'

'I? Oh no, no, no! Rita – she is only – how you say? – a matter of convenience. I jus' come for the trip weeth her. I so wish to see the so great city of the North America. All my life I hear an' read of New York. It ees the grand ambition of my life to come here. Rita, she 'ave the money. She give me the opportunity. But Rita, she know I do not love her. I tell her so. She ees ver' fine woman, but I do not love her.'

'Well suppose she found out you was up here with me all

afternoon. Do you think she'd resent it? What I mean is, do you think she'd get sore?'

'Oh, she would not like eet ver' much. She ees ver' jealous of you.'

'I suppose she told you I was a fast woman?'

'Ah, she talk, all the time talk, but I do not hear what she say – eet goes, how you say? – in one ear and out the nose!'

Lil laughed. 'You mean in your mouth and out your ear!'

'Yes, that ees it!'

'Well, anyway, I ain't got nothin' against Rita much, although I can't say I like her. Of course, I never did like to take a man away from a jane, but bein' you just explained that you ain't too intimate with her, that kinder clears my conscience.'

Juarez reached out an arm and drew her close to him. His lips brushed her ear.

'Tell me you care for me. Tell me I am more to you than other men. Say you 'ave not had so very many men. Eet 'urts me to theenk you 'ave love other men like you 'ave love me.'

'Well, I ain't had so *many* men. But those I had was good. How'd you think I got all my diamonds, playin' pinochle? You know they don't hand you out diamonds for just lookin' at them.'

'Oh, but now, now you have enough diamonds. You are made for love, and for love only you should care.'

Lil thrust out both arms and her eyes feasted upon her glittering wrists and fingers. Her face was lighted by a singular glow of pleasure. Her voice was almost hushed as she said:

'Diamonds is my career!'

The afternoon drew to a close, and while there was much she would like to have experimented with in the way of love, she felt, however reluctantly, that she really must be getting back to Gus's.

From her side she heard Juarez murmur:

'Many more like theese, and I no fight the bull.'

'Hell,' she said with a laugh. 'They was just rehearsal. Wait'll we put on the real act.'

'*Buenos Dios!*' Juarez exclaimed.

Lil rose and prepared to leave.

'Well, let that be all,' she said suddenly.

Juarez stiffened as though he had received an electric shock.

'All!' he cried. 'How you mean – all?'

Lil glanced over at him. 'You're complainin', ain'tcha? I don't want to wear you down all in one day. You can't be a hog at this thing. You got to use moderation!'

Juarez sprang up and commenced to help her with her stockings and shoes. She could have done far better without his help, for he kept interrupting the work to treat each leg to a series of kisses.

Lil laughed. 'You'd be a great guy to have around on Saturday nights.'

Juarez did not understand, but he laughed too.

'I want to be weeth you ever' night. I weel come to you ever' night.'

'No you won't,' Lil said firmly. 'I enjoy your company and all that. But I ain't gonna do nothin' to antagonize Gus.'

'But I weel see you tomorrow. I must see you tomorrow!'

'I ain't so sure about tomorrow.'

Juarez was visibly agitated.

'But why? Cannot we come here tomorrow?'

'I tell you I can't plan so far ahead. Besides, I ain't figgerin' on makin' a habit of this joint.'

'I leave ever'thing to you, my beautiful. But when ees eet that I may see you again and to hold you in my arms?'

'It's a toss-up,' she said. 'I'll have to let you know later.' She enjoyed Juarez's company, of that she was sure; but she had no desire to have him tagging her all over like a puppy. No matter how much she liked a guy, if he kept pushin' himself in her face all the time she wound up by treating him like a doormat. She liked to be the one to say 'Start!' and she usually knew when to say 'Stop!'

Lil was funny that way. She liked a guy better when he was hard to get. The other kind she used like an orange, squeezing it dry and tossing the skin into the handiest receptacle. She liked Juarez well enough to play the game with him, but she hoped he wouldn't prove to be the usual piece of fruit.

She moved to the door.

'I'm leavin' here alone. Just in case, see?'

Juarez rushed to her and seized her in his arms for a final kiss.

'I love you! I love you! I'm mad about you!' he cried pleadingly.

'All right,' she said. 'I'll see you later. Now run along home.'

He heard the rustle of her skirts as she slowly descended the stairs to the street.

10

A NIGHT IN DIVISION STREET

THERE was a time when Kitty would have crawled on her dimpled knees after Spot McGee, but now her search for the whining stool-pigeon was a different matter. She had been commissioned by Gus Jordan to execute a secret piece of investigation, and she felt very much like an ambassadress on her first day at the Court of St James, so important did she consider her mission. Anything that Gus Jordan commanded was as good as, even better than, law in the Bowery district. Like hundreds of others within the radius of Chatham Square, Kitty looked up to Gus as though he were a god on Olympus, capable of dealing out thunderbolts or ambrosia, according to his displeasure or pleasure.

Kitty had not seen Spot for many months, and she wondered if the sallow-faced panderer still flopped in Division Street. It was not so many years ago that as a pig-tailed kid she had excited Spot's lecherous instincts with her childish curiosity, and in no time at all he saw to it that there was nothing left to her imagination. The stork, as far as Kitty was concerned, was a winter's tale for children. Spot had made her a woman, and she adored the simple-minded yet cunning scum that he was.

At that time Spot McGee, though only in the early twenties, was old in the ways of cheap crime that rises out of dumb, unthinking, helpless poverty. He was also wise in the ways of making bartered flesh yield a profit.

It was not long before his first instinctive affection for Kitty acquired a commercial tinge. It took him a week to figure out a way to initiate her into whoredom, for even the moth-eaten soul of Spot McGee recognized a certain delicacy in swinging a girl from the particular to the general. He began by being excessively nice to her.

He took her to see the races at Gravesend, and while Kitty stood enthralled at the sport of kings he moved leisurely through the dense crowd amiably picking pockets with long, deft, cigarette-stained fingers. When he came back, his pockets stuffed with loot, he beamed on Kitty and commenced to point out various young ladies whom he claimed were getting rich by selling their charms to all and sundry that had the asking price. The fact that he had never seen those young ladies before, some of whom happened to be debutantes of the best families in New York, did not bother Spot one bit. They simply served him as a means of approach to the career he had planned for Kitty.

Kitty was somewhat incredulous, not believing that so much beauty and refinement and elegance could give itself promiscuously for money. Kitty, of course, was in love. She could not see in Spot the horrible caricature of a human being that he really was. She expressed her doubts.

'Why, Spot,' Kitty protested. 'Yer don't mean t' tell me them ladies is bad?'

Spot gave her a look of irritable impatience.

'Wha' d'ya mean – bad?' he said gratingly. 'It ain't bad to git rich, is it?'

'No,' Kitty had to admit, 'but it ain't right sleepin' wit' a different feller every night.'

'Who says?' Spot demanded.

'Well, them Salvation Army preachers say it ain't.'

'Oh,' sneered Spot. What d' them blokes know about it?

They ain't never tried it, has they? An' if you never tries a thing you never knows nuttin' about it, do yer?'

This sounded very logical to Kitty. She didn't want Spot to be angry with her for being so dull.

'I guess maybe you're right, Spot,' she agreed.

'O' course I'm right, honey,' said Spot. 'Say, listen, any time Spot McGee don't steer you right, you kin take an' bust me over the knob wit' a bung-starter. 'At's how sure I am, when I'm right.'

Spot didn't go on with the subject just then. He saw that Kitty had a picture implanted in her mind. He took her to Coney Island before he developed it.

They brought their lunch and lay about on the beach, got burned to the colour of boiled lobsters, and ate sandwiches and fruit that were gritty with sand. Again Spot looked about for an example to serve as an introduction for a discussion on the advantages of quick turnover when merchandising sex.

He saw a beautifully formed girl with red hair, who wore a bathing-suit that daringly revealed her bare ankles and elbows. She was the cynosure of all eyes on the beach – scornful feminine eyes, and hot, admiring masculine eyes.

'Now you see that girl?' Spot asked Kitty.

'Yeah,' said Kitty, munching a peach, 'she's makin' a holy show of herself in that bathin'-suit, ain't she?'

'Naw, naw,' Spot growled. 'Hell, I'm broadminded. That ain't what I mean a-tall. That gal is like them others I showed yer at Gravesend track. She's doin' a A-No. 1 business, makin' lots o' coin. Why, sometimes she gets fifty guys a day. Besides that, she's got a steady guy she's in love wit'.' Spot had never seen this girl before either.

Kitty's mouth fell open. Then her mouth snapped shut and she said with conviction:

'I could never do that.'

Spot gave her a sharp look and drew in a long breath and began:

'Now listen, honey. Yer don't understand. Yer see, it's this way. Yer know even the Bible says you ain't gotta letcha right hand know what yer left is doin'. Well, them fifty guys this here gal has don't mean nothin' to her. Why, sleepin' wit' them don't mean no more to 'er than shakin' hands. It's only the guy she loves what matters, see?'

Kitty shook her head pityingly.

'The poor feller,' she said.

'Wha' d'ya mean – poor feller?' Spot demanded.

'He don't know about it, does he?' Kitty inquired in surprise.

'Why, he's broadminded like me,' said Spot. 'He goes out and digs up them guys for her. Between 'em, workin' togedder like that, they makes lots o' coin an' they have grand times an' everythin'.'

Kitty lowered her eyes.

'You wouldn't want for me to do that, Spot, wouldja?'

'Sure. It'd be a great thing for us. Yer love me, don'tcha?'

'Yeah, I do. Lots,' said Kitty, 'but — '

'Now listen, Kit,' said Spot, putting an arm round her. 'Winter's comin' on and you're gonna need clothes an' things, an' this pickin' pockets business ain' what it used to be, yer know an' . . . '

And so they took a room in Division Street, and Spot added the trade of pimp to his other accomplishments. He handled the money, and for a year Kitty stuck it out. Generously, Spot would slip her a dollar now and then of the money she earned. When she grew too tired and worn to receive more than a handful of men a day, Spot left her for a plump, rosy-cheeked girl who could welcome fifty or so.

Kitty drifted about the Bowery until she hit Gus's 'Suicide Hall'. It was discovered that she had a pretty good voice, well adapted to sob songs, and Gus gave her a chance.

Occasionally, after her separation from Spot, she had run across him and they had spent a night or two together. She had really loved the gutter-rat. God knows why.

Tonight, on her way to Division Street, Kitty felt free of that tremendous hold Spot McGee had for so long exercised over her. She wasn't quite sure he was still living in the Division Street room. He had gone back to their room after she had left. And he had been living there up to the time she had last seen him some months previous.

From the street she glanced up at the windows of the room, which was a front one. She was not sure, but there seemed to be a little light coming through chinks in the drawn blinds. She mounted the stairs to the top floor and knocked on the door. The hallway smelt of mice and dinners long gone. Presently, as she waited, she heard the stirring of someone inside the room and the crazy whine and creak which told her that the old familiar bed was occupied. She knocked sharply again.

'What the hell you want?' a voice, which Kitty at once recognized as Spot's, demanded.

'It's Kitty. Open up, Spot.'

Again she heard the bed's protesting voice, and an instant later the door was flung open. Spot was wearing a nightshirt that fluttered about the calves of his legs in the sudden draught occasioned by the opened door. His hair was tousled and his face puffy from sleep and perhaps from the liquor, the odour of which enveloped Kitty when he spoke to her. He wasn't at all a pleasant sight, and Kitty smiled and felt very superior, and wondered why she had ever thought she loved him.

'Come on in, honey,' invited Spot. She followed him into the drab room. Over the only available chair Spot's pants were draped grotesquely. Kitty sat on the edge of the bed while Spot poured himself three fingers of whisky. 'Have a drink,' he offered.

'Nope,' said Kitty. 'You look as if you been rummin' it up pretty lively. What's a matter?'

'Not a goddam thing,' said Spot, tossing off the drink. 'Does a guy have to have a excuse for takin' a drink?'

Kitty smiled to herself.

'You sure this stoolin' ain't gettin' on yer nerves?'

Spot gave a start and turned on her.

'What give you that idea? Why should I worry? Ain't it right to help out the law?'

Kitty laughed.

'Yeah. But that's what they got cops for. There's a lot o' folks can't see why a ordinary citizen should go givin' 'em information.'

Spot poured himself another drink, a stiffer one than the last. When he had downed it he came over and sat beside her on the bed.

'Well, is this a little visit like the last one, or what?' he asked her.

'A little visit, yeah,' she returned. 'But not like the last one.'

'You used to like me a lot, Kit,' he said. 'We had a lotta fun, didn't we?'

'You mean *you* did,' Kitty told him.

'I admit I coulda done a heap better by you, honey, but – oh, what the hell, life's too damn' short to worry about whatcha done and whatcha maybe gonna do. We're still pals, ain't we?'

'Sure, Spot,' said Kitty, bearing her mission in mind. 'I ain't holdin' nothin' against you.'

'That's the way I like to hear you talk, baby,' he rejoined, taking out a cigarette and lighting it.

'What's the news around town, Spot?' Kitty inquired.

'Well, for one thing, these here lousy reformers is certain'y diggin' up plenty o' dirt on the city administration.'

'Yeah,' said Kitty, 'I been hearin' about that. Been puttin' in some special investigators, I hear, 'caus they say there's too much graft in the police department.'

'Well,' drawled Spot, 'I wouldn't say that exackly. You know people talk. Why, there's plenty o' honest cops around this town.'

'Where, in the cemetery?'

'Aw, now listen,' protested Spot. 'What good is all this reformin' gonna do? It's gonna make it harder to earn a livin' for lots o' people.'

'What about a big man like Gus Jordan?' Kitty asked.

'Him too,' said Spot. 'If the reformers git in they'll put him out o' business. It stands to reason. Gus's been gettin' away wit' some pretty raw stuff.'

'How d'you mean?' Kitty wanted to be told. 'He ain't pullin' nothin' worse than the Bucket of Blood or Nigger Mike's.'

'Oh, ain't he?' Spot snorted derisively.

'What then?' Kitty demanded.

'If I knowed just what I could collect some nice new coin for meself. But they got their eyes on him, I'm tellin' yer.'

Kitty feigned astonishment.

'I don't believe it!' she exclaimed. 'You're makin' it up.'

'The hell I am!' Spot cried indignantly. 'Don'tcha think I know the inside on this town? Don't I know there's a new dick around, specially detailed from headquarters to keep givin' Gus an' his place the up an' down?'

Kitty gasped.

'A special dick?'

'Certain'y. He's a mysterious sort o' duck. Nobody seems to know his name, or they ain't givin' out for publication or somethin', but anyways, the boys tell me he's supposed to be smart. They call him "The Hawk".'

'The Hawk? Why, 'cause he likes chickens or somethin'?'

Spot gave her a disgusted look that almost said: 'How can anybody be so dumb and live?'

'They call him the Hawk,' he explained laboriously, 'because he's been raidin' places right an' left. He pounces down on 'em unexpected like and gits 'em red-handed. This is sure gettin' to be a hell of a town. There was a time the cops would tip yer off when they was goin' to raid yer. But now everythin's tightened up on account o' these here reformers. It's terrible.'

'You sure you don't know who this here Hawk is, Spot? I'm dyin' o' curiosity. Tell me, Spot. You know I'm on the level, an' . . .'

'Jeez, ain't I just got through tellin' you I ain't never even seen the bloke, no less knowin' his moniker? It's got me sore. How kin I do business if I don't know everythin' goin' on this hole of a town?'

'You're just tryin' to keep me guessin',' said Kitty. 'Come on, tell me. You used to tell me lots o' things when we was sleepin' together.'

'Oh, I was reckless in them days.'

'Aw, come on, Spot. I can keep a secret. You know I never open my mouth.'

'No. No wider than the Brooklyn Bridge!'

Whether Spot knew or didn't know who 'The Hawk' was, that was all Kitty could get out of him.

11

LIL GETS SOME HOT NEWS

LIL made it a point to avoid Juarez after her episode with him in the Elizabeth Street room. Several days had now passed and she had not seen him. She had no doubt that he was hovering around every day, watching for her to go forth in her cab, but she had not gone out except a couple of times in the evening with Gus to the Bowery Theatre to see *Nellie, the Beautiful Cloak Model* and *East Lynne*. He had not appeared at night with Rita.

She had been extra nice to Gus after trespassing the forbidden path with the ardent Juarez. Gus had been extraordinarily good to her, and she experienced certain qualms of conscience – a thing she never thought she had – over her unfaithfulness. Nevertheless, she knew she would do the same thing again. Calmly she calculated that in a few more days, when Juarez was seething like a volcano after his prolonged and enforced abstinence from the delights of her love, she would have him again. Then once more she would return to Gus temporarily contrite and be extra nice to him. Lil could be bothered with a conscience only just so long. But she felt that to be a repentant sinner one must first have something to repent.

Had she not heard the Salvation Army preacher say that there is 'more joy in Heaven over a sinner who repenteth' than over somebody who was good because he was afraid to be bad? Lil was even acquainted with the parable of the Pharisee and the Publican, in which the humble repentance of the Publican was much preferred to the Pharisee's boasting of virtue.

Yes, Lil had read the Bible, and read it with interest. Her blood had been curdled by the tale of John the Baptist and how he lost his head because Salome, Princess of Judea, lusted after his body and he had refused it to her. She had read, too, of the Great Whore of Babylon and the other terrors in the Book of Revelation.

She liked the stalwart David, who slew Goliath, and she adored Solomon, who sang so wonderfully of his love for Sulamith. Lil loved the robust, the sensuous, the strong. The pale Nazarene and his doctrine of self-abnegation were too meek and mild for her. She liked best the Old Testament, whose men and women were of the earth, mighty in war and mighty in love. She could not understand Job's patience, and Moses was nothing more to her than a magician. She did not doubt, though, that Jonah had actually managed to live in a whale's belly. Samson intrigued her. He was all man. Delilah, Lil could sympathize with, because she had clipped more than one strong man herself.

This morning she had slept late and was just completing her toilet when a knock came at her bedroom door.

'Come in,' she called, knowing it would either be Gus or one of the girls. As a matter of fact, it was three. Frances, Flo and Kitty fluttered in, bringing with them a gush of cheap perfume. Each was carrying a paper parcel.

'Hello, Lil!' they chorused.

Lil greeted them in off-hand fashion and they plumped themselves down wherever it was convenient. They were all set for a good talk. Lil was prepared to let them enjoy themselves, for they often furnished her a good laugh.

The girls were distinct types. Frances had the face of a

Dresden doll and her hair, thick and braided about her head, was what is vulgarly known as dirty blonde. Her round blue eyes had an innocent look. Lil had told her that they were the only innocent thing about her.

Kitty's hair had been a carrot-red, but she had darkened it, because there are always people who take the fun out of life by bestowing nicknames on everyone who has some noticeable feature. They had called her 'Brick-top'. She couldn't care for it. She had a pert nose that made her look fresh, and she was fresh.

Flo had hair that was as black as the inside of a clothes-press, and lots of it. Her eyes were large, black velvet patches in a white oval. Her mouth was like a cut that had bled a little. A dozen freckles paraded across the bridge of her nose. Her voice was ginny.

'We've been shoppin', Lil,' said Frances complacently, holding up her package.

'Yeah?' Lil said with a smile. 'I thought maybe you'd brung your lunch. What you got there?'

Frances opened her parcel and unfurled a white lace corset-cover. She held it out to Lil.

'Ain't dat de frog's warts?' she said, as Lil took it and held it round her.

'Kinder pretty,' Lil told her. 'Where'd you lift this from?'

'Maxer's,' replied Frances, working her jaws on a piece of chewing-wax.

'You're gettin' better an' better,' Lil commented. 'You're beginnin' to pick out the expensive stuff. It don't pay to lift cheap articles. You gotta learn to discriminate.'

The girls looked at one another.

'What d'you mean, Lil?' Flo inquired. 'You don't mean somethin' dirty, do yer?'

'Jeeze!' said Lil. 'Can't I ever learn you nothin'? You girls got to increase your vocab – vocab – well, anyway, you gotta learn how to use more words if you want to carry on a intelligent conversation. It's the only way you'll ever get guys who was smart enough to get past the kindergarten.'

'Well, what does that word you said mean, Lil?' Kitty was anxious to learn.

'You mean discriminate? Why, that just means, if you can discriminate, then you can tell what's best from what's rotten. You got good taste then.'

'You mean you should taste everything before you swipe it?' asked Flo. 'Like you bite a quarter to see if it dents?'

Lil sighed.

'Let it pass. I might only confuse you.'

The girls also sighed, with relief. It was too much for them.

Kitty untied her package and removed a half dozen pairs of black silk stockings. She displayed them proudly.

'You ain't done so bad neither,' Lil remarked, thrusting her hand inside a stocking so that she could test the fineness of it. 'That's good stuff. Where'd you pick these up, Kitty?'

'Maxer's,' said Kitty. 'I like to go there. They got such nice things. You got such a big choice.'

'Yeah.' said Lil dryly. 'Guess you was sorry you didn't have a wagon with you. Remember what I told you girls. Don't get careless. Just take a little at a time. And don't all go into a place together. What did you come off with, Flo?'

'Wait'll you see this, Lil,' Flo declared eagerly, breaking the strings of her package.

Lil looked from one to the other.

'You all got these things wrapped up. Don't tell me you had 'em done up in the store?'

'Oh no!' they chorused.

'We tied 'em up ourselves after we got away,' said Frances. 'Gawd, Lil, you learned us better'n 'at.'

Flo was holding up a fur neck-piece between thumb and finger. 'Ain't that splendiferous?' she cried.

Lil took the fur-piece in her hands and looked at it critically.

'It's a nice piece of skunk,' Lil said. 'But it ain't exactly my style. I been thinkin' of gettin' me some ermine. 'Course, bein' as how Gus just gimme a new ring, I don't want to ast him just now. But can you pitcher, girls – diamonds and ermine together! What a combination!'

They not only could picture it, but did, and gasped at the idea.

Lil handed the fur-piece back to Flo, who drew it round her neck. It seemed ever so small and ever so shabby after Lil's talk of ermine.

'Why,' said Flo, 'I thought only kings and queens wore ermine.'

Well, said Lil, 'you know they ain't got exclusive right to wear it. If you janes ever went to the Haymarket you'd see enough of it to carpet this joint up to your navel.

The girls screamed with laughter.

'Can you 'magine?' shrieked Frances.

'Well,' said Lil, taking a cigarette and making herself comfortable on the swan bed, 'any of you girls fell in love lately? That's a bad habit you got, an' I can't seem to break you of it. But what's new around? I been so busy, I been kinder out of touch.'

'Oh, Frances has got a new flame,' said Flo. 'She's been keepin' him in her room for a week. Afraid somebody'd get their hooks on 'im.'

'It mightn't be such a bad procedure at that,' Lil commented. 'What is it – love this time? Or just the usual business?'

'I guess I'm kinder dippy about him,' Frances admitted.

Lil exhaled a thin plume of smoke.

'You go gettin' in love and the first thing you know you'll be a two-bit tart with cut-rates for Chinks. Fallin' in love gets you that way. Yer brains get jellied. Time to think o' love is when yer gettin' too old to keep up your prices.'

Frances lowered her eyes, and the other girls looked at her. Lil laughed good-naturedly.

'There ain't no use of me tellin' this, I guess. Nobody takes advice. I even forget to take my own sometimes.'

Frances felt better, and giggled.

'Maybe you're right, Lil. Maybe I will end up in a garbage-can, but bein' in love has got a lot to it.'

'Yeah. So I imagine,' said Lil. She breathed on the nails of her right hand and polished them in the palm of her left. Her eyes swept around, taking in all the girls before she continued. 'In this business,' she went on, 'you don't get no place 'less you takes yer head to bed with yer, same as the rest of yer. Now you're the kind o' janes that leaves yer head on a chair with yer duds.'

There was a silence for a moment, and then Kitty spoke.

'Who d'you think I seen the other night?'

'I couldn't guess,' said Lil.

'Spot McGee,' Kitty told her.

'Oh,' said Lil. 'That's the crab-apple who took you for a toboggan a while back, ain't it?'

'Yeah, Lil,' Kitty sighed. 'I'm still kinder soft on him.'

'How is the louse?' Lil inquired.

'He ain't lost none o' his style, Lil.'

'Better not be hangin' around with no stoolie. That'll getcha in trouble,' Lil warned. She saw Kitty's face fall. 'Well, anyway,' she added, 'don't go sleepin' in no draughts with him an' I guess you'll be all right.'

Kitty brightened up with a new thought.

'Say, Lil, have yer lamped the new Salvation Army captain?'

Lil hesitated. She showed no interest.

'No,' she lied. 'Can't say as I have. What's the matter with him?'

'Nothin',' Kitty asserted. 'That's just it. He's so good-lookin', he makes you ache all over just to look at him.'

'Now, that sounds like somethin',' Lil said. 'Tell me about him.'

'I only just seen him a while ago,' Kitty said. 'He was givin' out circulars around the Square, tellin' about the meetin's they're holdin' every night in Jacobsen's Hall. He gimme one, and when he did he says, 'Come and be saved, sister, come and be saved.' He's got such wonderful eyes.'

'Yeah,' said Lil, 'an' you felt like goin' to heaven right then and there.'

'I tell you Lil, I reely did.'

'Sure,' said Lil. 'Just goes to show that religion'd be more of a success if they had better-lookin' people sellin' it. Who the hell can get worked up about goin' to a heaven where they's a lot o' people lookin' like they was brung up on a dill pickle? Now I ask yer!'

Frances rolled her blue-china eyes at Lil.

'They do say, Lil, that Jacobsen's Hall is jammed every night since the captain started holdin' meetin's there. Mostly women there, too.'

'Sure,' Lil retorted. 'A lot o' broken-down hustlers. The only fun they get out o' life now is weepin' for the sins they forgot to commit.'

The girls laughed at that.

Lil rose from the bed and, crossing to her mirror, arranged her hair a bit.

'I'm going downstairs,' she announced.

The girls drifted towards the door.

'I got to step out and do a little hustlin' today,' Flo said.

'Well, good luck,' Lil returned. 'And don't give 'em too much for their money.'

'So long,' the girls chorused, and went noisily down the stairs.

Lil gave a last glance at herself in the mirror, a last pat to her hair, and followed them. The dance-hall was empty, but there was a crowd in the bar.

Steak McGarry saw her over the top of the swinging doors and came in from the bar.

'Howya, Lil?' Steak greeted her.

'Hello, Steak,' Lil replied. 'How was the fight last night?'

'Rotten,' said Steak, making a face of disgust.

'Yeah?' queried Lil. 'What was the matter?'

'Oh, it was awright up t'de seventy-seventh round, then de bum got yeller an' quit!'

'Yeah, I guess fighters ain't what they used to be,' Lil commented. 'What's doin' around? Anythin'?'

'Just the reg'lar noon bunch stuffin' theirselves full o' free lunch,' said Steak.

All at once there was a crash of glass in the bar, a fearful rumpus ensued, and above the tumult could be heard a voice shrieking: 'I been robbed! I been robbed I tell yer! I been robbed!'

'Gosh! That guy's got a big voice,' said Lil.

Steak bolted into the bar.

'Hey, Bill!' Lil called to the powerful bartender.

'What d'you want?' came Bill's voice above the clamour.

'Give that bum his car fare, and tell him how lucky he is!' Lil cried.

The racket increased for a moment, as the complaining customer was booted out on the pavement of Chatham Square.

Chuck came in through the swinging doors, a newspaper in his hand, the ever-present cigar stuck in a corner of his mouth.

'I hoid yer voice, Lil,' he said. 'I thought maybe you'd like to see this.' He handed her the paper.

A huge black headline undulated like a snake across the white expanse of paper.

'Chick Clark!' she exclaimed involuntarily.

'Yeah,' said Chuck, and went out the side door into the street.

Rapidly Lil ran her eyes down the column of neat black type.

CHICK CLARK ESCAPES FROM STATE PEN

'Chicago' Chick Clark, notorious jewel thief and gunman of the Mid-west metropolis, escaped last night from the Illinois State Penitentiary at Joliet, as he was being removed from his old cell to one in the new cell block recently completed.

He stabbed his guard, John Lloyd, with a spoon that had been worn down to the sharpness of a stilleto. The weapon was left in the body of Lloyd, who it is believed may die of his wound.

Clark had been regarded as a model prisoner and vigilance had consequently been relaxed. It is believed the escaped convict is headed East to a hideaway in New York. The police here are on the lookout for him.

Clark, after wounding and knocking his guard unconscious, it is believed, made his way out unlocking intervening doors with the guard's keys.

12

◆◇◆

THE 'HALLELUJAH' MAN

THE news of Chick Clark's escape from prison fell upon Lil like a wet blanket. The hint, or rather the suspicion, conveyed in the news story that Clark was headed for New York was anything but pleasant reading for Diamond Lil. She knew Chick too well to think for a minute that her cast-off lover would be willing to let bygones be bygones. Chick was a dangerous man when he had any grievances, and Lil was ready to believe that he would consider her desertion of him a very sore one.

She did not regret for a moment that she had ditched Chick. She had bettered herself materially, at least. What was a mere man when weighed in the balance with the power and glory of glittering carats? As for a man's flesh' – why, the world was a stockyard of prize studs!

But Chick Clark didn't hesitate at killing to gain his ends. The newspaper account of his disposal of the guard was sufficient proof, if nothing else.

And he was coming! Coming East! She felt even more certain than the police and the newspapers that it was true. She knew that inevitably an hour of reckoning with him would come. But when? When? Probably when she least expected it.

The realization was not pleasant. But she told herself that

when the time came she wouldn't lose her nerve. She had a wonderful faith in her ability to handle any situation. But just the same, the news that Chick was free gave her a queer thrill. She didn't like complications.

She folded the paper carefully, figuring to take it to her room for a more careful reading later.

Spider Kane came in from the bar. He pulled up short when he saw Lil, and quickly removed his derby hat.

'Hello, Lil,' he said.

"Lo, Spider,' Lil replied absently.

Kane saw her knitted brows and the vague look in her eyes. From her face his glance drifted down to the paper in her hands. He frowned. He had seen the news, too.

'Anything the matter, Lil?' he inquired, sending her that frank look of adoration he always had for her.

'No,' said Lil. Unconsciously she twisted the paper in her hands.

Kane came closer. 'Now I know somethin's the matter. Listen, Lil – you always been a square-shooter wit' me, an' I ain't no double-crosser meself, but take a tip from me and watch that guy Dan Flynn. He's dangerous!'

Lil looked surprised.

'What, Flynn? Since when?'

'He's been busy, Lil, here an' there in the district.'

'Oh, you mean he's tryin' to get some of Gus's votes, or what?'

'Worse'n 'at, Lil. He's — ' But Kane was looking past Lil's shoulder and he broke off. 'I'll tell you 'bout it later, Lil,' he said hurriedly, and walked out to the bar.

Lil stared after Kane for a moment, wondering at his sudden exit, and then she decided she would return to her room and read about Chick Clark undisturbed. As she turned to go up the stairs she came face to face with the handsome Captain Cummings of the Salvation Army, whose face and figure had been present in many of her dreams of late.

Her eyes swept him from head to foot, and she thought that this time distance did not lend enchantment to the view, but that he was actually better to behold close up.

He removed his uniform cap and stared at her uncertainly. He made as if to speak, but for some unknown reason checked himself.

A rather scornful smile curled Lil's full lips.

'Well, look me over but don't try to reform me. 'Cause I hate made-over things.'

He looked her full in the eyes a moment.

'I didn't come here to see you,' he said clearly.

Lil rested her hand on the newel-post of the stairs.

'You don't have to confess anything. We don't deal in confessions here.'

The captain moved a trifle nearer. He seemed more sure of himself.

'Affects your conscience, perhaps. The uniform of salvation has been known to have that effect.'

'Say, I ain't got no conscience,' Lil snapped. 'You just come in here to look me over, to decide on what angle to start savin' my soul.'

'You mean, you are afraid that's why I came here?' he demanded coolly.

'I ain't afraid of nothin',' Lil said sharply.

'You're very fortunate indeed, Diamond Lil. You are Diamond Lil, aren't you?'

'Who'd you think I was, Mary Magdalene?'

'Please,' he said. 'I wasn't being sarcastic. I just wanted to make sure. Since you are Diamond Lil, I want to thank you on behalf of the army for the contributions you have made from time to time. You've been very generous and I know that the poor souls who benefited by your acts of kindness are very grateful — '

'Say, listen,' Lil interrupted. 'You'll have me sobbin' in a minute. What I give the army so far ain't nothin' to what

I'd give 'em if they'd stop psalm-singin' under my window when I'm tryin' to sleep.'

'I'm sorry if we disturb you. But we are trying to do God's work.'

'Well, can't you do it just as good a couple o' blocks away?'

Captain Cummings shook his head disapprovingly.

'You should not speak disrespectfully of God and those who serve Him.'

'All I'm interested in is Greek gods,' Lil asserted. 'You know, you kinder look like one yourself.'

The captain flushed madly.

'Please,' he protested. 'I didn't come here to have my person discussed.'

Lil looked up from under her lids.

'It ain't no sin to be handsome, is it?'

There was the sound of a slamming door, a rush of feet, and Pete the Duke burst in upon them, panting, dishevelled and wild-eyed. He was an habitué of Gus's; a thin, wiry, ferret-faced lad; a petty thief, pickpocket and snow-bird, who had got the nickname of 'The Duke' because of his extravagant talk when he was coked up higher than a kite.

He threw himself in front of Captain Cummings, and, cring-ing and trembling with fear, he clutched at the Salvationist. Altogether at once a pitiful and nauseating sight.

'Don't tell him I'm here!' he whined. 'For God's sake don't! Help me, Captain! Help me!'

The captain seized Pete the Duke by the shoulders and shook him gently.

'Here, here, Pete! Pull yourself together. What is it? What's the matter?'

'There was a window broken in Zeider's drug store,' he whimpered. 'Captain, I'd break into hell for some of the stuff right now!'

Beyond the side door to the street a deep harsh voice could be heard shouting, 'Which way did he go?'

Pete almost fainted with fear.

'That's Doheny now!' he cried. 'Don't let him get me, Captain! Don't let him get me!'

Lil looked on impassively. The incident was nothing new in her experience.

'Here, be quiet,' Cummings commanded. He looked about quickly, and seeing the door to a lavatory marked 'Gents', he shoved Pete towards it. 'Go in there and keep perfectly still.'

Lil grinned openly. 'He'll die in there if he has to stay long. That ain't no conservatory.'

Cummings gave her an aggrieved look, but before he could make a reply the side door to the street opened and a huge bull neck and red face topped by a grey felt helmet and thick body swathed in blue broadcloth barged in. That was Officer Doheny.

'Well, where is he?' demanded Doheny, with his usual cocksureness.

'What's the matter, Doheny?' the captain inquired calmly.

Doheny's red face became tinged with purple.

'Don't try to kid me. I know that you army people are always tryin' to save these dirty dopes. Where'd he go? Where'd you put him?'

Cummings's voice took on a tone of annoyance.

'What is it, Doheny? What's happened?'

Doheny gritted his teeth.

'Now listen. I got the goods on him and got him right.'

The captain seemed amazed.

'The goods? On who?'

'Who? Pete the Duke, that's who!' he fumed. 'I heard that glass crash and he came running out of the alley and headed straight for here.'

The captain glanced at Lil and then turned coolly to the irate officer.

'Wait a moment, Doheny,' he said. 'How could it be

possible for him to run out of the alley and down here if he has been helping me all afternoon?'

Doheny almost burst a blood-vessel.

'Who said so?' he roared. 'Who said so? Will you go before a judge and swear to that?' He shook his club furiously.

Lil stirred lazily.

'Sure he would,' she drawled, 'and so would I. Two against one, Doheny, so flap your heels.' She suppressed a yawn daintily behind a hand.

Doheny exploded. He wheeled on Cummings.

'Now let me tell you somethin',' he bellowed. 'You're goin' to git yourself in a lot o' trouble tryin' to be a saint for these dirty bums. Take my word fer it, it ain't goin' to git you nothin' from nobody!'

The captain's voice was calmly soothing.

'Listen, Doheny,' he said, 'if you and I could work together we could prevent a lot of suffering. We could help these poor wretches.'

Doheny snorted in derision.

'Help them? There's only one way to help thim divils! Take the stuff away from thim, lock 'em up and keep 'em where they can't git any more.'

Cummings's reply was sharp.

'Doheny, what about the pedlars that start them on the habit? Turn them loose, eh?'

The policeman's eyes dropped to the floor.

'I don't know what yer mean. Show me anyone that breaks the law, prove it, and I'll lock them up.'

The door to Jordan's office was flung open violently and Gus himself strode in.

'What's the matter here?' he demanded angrily. He shot a glowering look at the captain. 'Oh, I thought the army gave up the idea of tryin' to reform this place.'

Cummings turned to him coolly.

'We soldiers of the army are still hopeful, Mr Jordan.'

'Hopeful hell!' Gus said with a snort. 'People see you comin' in here, they'll think I'm runnin' a Sunday-school and give me the go-by.'

He jammed his cigar between his teeth, returned to his office and slammed the door behind him.

Lil smiled to herself and mounted the stairs a step or two.

The captain had more to say to Doheny.

'How about Johnnie the Pup? We gave you proof last week. You didn't lock him up. Snow-bird Robbins is still running free.'

Doheny stiffened as though he had received a jolt on the chin.

'What are you drivin' at?' he snarled. 'Are you tryin' to say I took a bribe?'

Lil gave him a laugh.

'Why, we wouldn't think of sayin' such a thing.'

The copper, who found himself in deep water, shook his baton at the Salvationist.

'You tend to your Bible-readin' and I'll tend to my business.'

'That's right, Doheny,' the captain told him, 'you save their bodies and I'll save their souls.'

'Save their — ' Doheny choked. 'Oh, hell! What's the use!'

He stormed out into the street.

For an instant the captain relaxed. He looked discouraged.

Lil watched him in silence for a moment. Then:

'Not having much luck, are you?' she asked.

Cummings shook his head.

'I'd have a great deal more if Doheny and the others would co-operate.'

Lil leaned an elbow on the newel-post and cupped her chin in the palm of her hand.

'Ain't none of them worth saving,' she said evenly. 'You keep hanging around long enough and you'll be that way yourself.'

He came towards her.

'Thanks for your kind interest,' he said. 'But that's not for us to worry about. We're in the hands of God. He'll take care of us.'

'I ain't never met the gentleman,' said Lil.

'Well, perhaps I can bring you two together,' he said seriously.

'It wouldn't do you no good,' Lil assured him.

'But it would do *you* good,' he declared.

Lil drew herself erect.

'I don't want to be good,' she told him.

The captain looked properly shocked.

'Oh, I read your Bible,' Lil said. 'A lot of it's about me. I'm the scarlet woman. When I die, I'm goin' to burn in hell. All right. That's me. That's how I live; that's how I die. No crawfishin' for me.'

He came close to her protestingly.

'Oh, but you do want to be good,' he asserted. 'And the good will come to the top, if you'll only give it half a chance.'

Lil ignored his good counsel. Her hand went out and rested on his shoulder. Her lids dropped slightly and her eyes sought his sideways through the long fringe of her lashes. That look was the epitome of all sensuousness.

'You know, I always like a man in uniform' – in a tone that fairly breathed forbidden things. 'That one fits you perfect. Say, why don't you come up some time? I'm home every evening.'

She leaned towards him. Her breasts curved voluptuously beneath his eyes. He drew back with a quick intake of breath.

'I – I'm sorry,' he stammered. 'But – but I'm busy every evening.'

Lil stiffened. 'Busy? Say, are you trying to insult me?'

Captain Cummings was vastly confused. His masterful air and poise seemed suddenly to have evaporated.

'Why, not at all,' he assured her 'I – I'm just busy, that's all. You see, we're holding meetings in Jacobsen's Hall every evening. Any time you have a few minutes to spare we'd like to have you come in. You're more than welcome.'

Lil smiled ravishingly.

'I heard you,' she said. 'But you don't fool me, pretendin' to be good. I've met your kind before.' Once more she leaned towards him and her hips moved suggestively. 'Why don't you come up some time, hmm?'

Captain Cummings began to back towards the door; he could not take his eyes from her. She held him with the fascination that a certain snake has for a rabbit.

'Don't be afraid,' she coaxed. 'I won't tell.'

By that time he was at the door. Her voice followed him.

'Now, you can be had,' she said with a musical laugh.

The captain fled.

13

FOR A WOMAN

As night smeared its obliterating black pitch over the colours of earth, making all one with its shadows, Chick crawled from under the hayrick in the field where he had lain all day. Since the first light of dawn he had been burrowed in like a fieldmouse.

He rose to his full height in the safe darkness and stretched his cramped muscles. His empty stomach ached like a wound and he tightened the belt of his prison dungarees. He threshed his hair with his fingers, endeavouring to get the hayseed out of it. He filled his lungs with the night air fragrant with meadow-sweet, and let it out softly, noiselessly.

For a moment then he listened intently. Only the chatter of crickets and the puttering of a cow in the pasture beyond came to his ears. He smiled and rubbed his unshaven chin.

Since his escape the night before he had covered only fifteen miles. He had run till he was exhausted, attempting to put as many miles behind him as possible before dawn caught up with him. Twice he had lain in the underbrush and heard the chase go by. Because of his prison garb he had not dared to venture forth during the day that followed. But now with darkness conspiring to help him and his own good luck holding out he'd try to get to 'Tiny Jo' Breslin's 'safety' farm.

He stood still for several minutes trying to get his bearings.

Over there a half-mile were the lights of a farmhouse. He had come that way. The road must be across the field in front of him. He would turn to his left and walk till he came to a cross-roads. There would be a house there, he had been told, with a white pump in the front yard. Hell, he'd be able to see that even in the dark. He'd have to walk past the front of the house and follow that road about four miles. Then he'd be at Tiny Jo's.

Chick's eyes were growing used to the blackness. He stumbled across the field till a stone fence brought him up short. He listened and, satisfied that the coast was clear, climbed the fence and dropped on to the road. He began to walk, keeping to the edge of the road in the fringe of blueberry bushes and lilac shrubs that grew by the roadside in profusion.

His ears were strained to bursting for any untoward sound. He halted now and again at some unfamiliar sound, and was not satisfied to go on till he had isolated the sound and knew the nature of it.

A half-hour's walking brought him to the cross-roads. The white pump in the yard of the house stuck out in the darkness like a bandaged thumb. He plodded on, sure of his direction now. His stomach ached miserably. He wondered what Tiny Jo would have in his ice-box. Even more than his hunger he felt the need of tobacco. A cigarette he wanted first of all. In the back of his mind was the body of a woman. But she would only come to the forefront of his thoughts after he had filled his belly.

The miles seemed endless. His eyes ached from straining them in the darkness. Curses flooded to his lips but became meaningless mumblings. The effort needed to tear them out of his throat was too great for his already over-exerted body. He felt at the moment no exultation at his freedom. He had planned. He had waited. He had seized his opportunity, and here he was. Effect had followed cause very nicely.

Presently, to his left ahead, about fifty yards back from the road, he saw his destination. He could not mistake it. He had been there on two previous occasions. Happier ones, however, than this.

He leaned on the gate-post for a moment looking up the path that led to the front door. From a side window there was a faint projection of light. The gate creaked rustily as he swung it open and moved on up the path. As he neared the veranda he diverged, and, not being like Brutus, an 'honourable man', he went round to the side of the house and peered in at the window.

There were three men seated at a table playing cards. Two had their backs to him, but Tiny Jo, who, by the way, was six feet three inches, faced him. In the broad Irish face with its coarse nose, beetling brows and sulky mouth was stuck a clay pipe that gave forth a blue ribbon of smoke every time the smoker breathed.

Chick grinned at the scene, and then, stopping, he groped around for a second, came up with a few pebbles and flung them at the window-pane. With amusement he watched Tiny Jo give a start and then rise from the table. Breslin took the lamp and came to the window.

Chick thrust his face close to the pane so that the light of the lamp fell full upon him. He heard Tiny Jo exclaim: 'Bejasus!' Then the big man with the little name started for the front door. Chick went round and crossed the veranda. In a moment a huge hand had seized his and drawn him inside.

'Mother o' God!' cried Tiny Jo Breslin. 'Thin the papers wuz right fer oncet! Chick, me lad, I'm glad ye're clear o' that blasted hell-hole. Come in, they's none but pals here.'

'Gimme a cigarette, Tiny,' Chick Clark said. 'And then somethin' to eat. My belly feels like my throat's cut!'

'Sure, an' you'll git all ye want in two shakes of a lamb's tail. Sit down at the table with the b'ys.'

They passed into the room where the men had been playing cards. Chick squinted in the light of the lamp at the two men who remained seated but with their eyes fixed on him.

Then one of them jumped up and held out his hand.

'You knows Slink Mehaffey,' said Tiny Jo to Chick.

'Sure. Sure,' said Chick, taking Mehaffey's hand. 'Howya, pal?'

'Nice job,' said Slink. He turned to the other man, a dapper, well-kept person with small black eyes, black hair carefully parted and slicked down, black moustache carefully waxed, and hands as soft and white as a woman's. He was dressed in the height of fashion.

'This is Barney Bledso, Chick,' Slink introduced. 'You heard o' each other I guess.'

'Sure, sure,' said Chick. 'Glad to meetcha.'

'I've always admired your work, Clark,' said Bledso in an educated voice that was as soft and smooth as a woman's breast. 'I'm delighted to make your acquaintance.'

Chick knew Bledso to be one of the slickest grifters in the country. As a confidence man Blarney Bledso could sell a man his own overcoat right off his back.

'Sit down, man, by all means,' said Bledso. He tilted a bottle and poured a glass of brandy. 'Here, get that into your stomach as a start. And a cigarette. I heard you ask for one.' He extended a box to Chick.

'Thanks,' Chick replied 'Cripes! That's good!' he exclaimed at the first inhalation of smoke. He looked around. 'Where the hell's Tiny with the grub?'

'He's gettin' it,' said Slink.

Chick tossed off the brandy. It eased down his dusty throat and sent a pleasant glow of warmth through his hollow stomach. His mind began to sharpen immediately.

'Leaving these parts pretty pronto, I take it?' Bledso inquired.

'You're damned well right,' said Chick. 'I'm going East.'

'Quite a coincidence,' said the confidence man. 'So am I. Tomorrow morning. Got any plans? I suppose you're going to New York and lay low for a while?'

Chick's eyes narrowed.

'Yeah. There's a couple o' things I got to do there.'

'I see,' said Bledso. 'Perhaps I might be able to help you out. I've got a place there where you'll be safe.'

'That'd be great,' said Chick. 'I'm hard up for coin right now. But when I gets to N'York I know where there's some ice I can get my hands on.'

Bledso nodded.

'Well, if you do, I know where you can cash in on it.'

'That's perfect,' said Chick. 'I'm much obliged to yer, Bledso.'

'That's all right. Always glad to help out a friend in the profession,' he smiled.

'Say,' said Chick, as a thought struck him. But Tiny Jo came in with a platter of cold chicken, white bread and a pot of coffee. Chick tore into it without another word. The others watched him eat.

'Go slow, me b'y,' cautioned Tiny Jo. 'Don't go overloadin' yer belly after fastin' so long. Jabers, thim bastard screws up to Joliet must keep yez short o' vittles!'

'Well,' said Chick, with a mouth full of food, 'I left one brass-buttoned son of a gun with a chiv in his guts. I don't know, though. For a screw, Johnnie Lloyd wasn't such a bad lug at that. I'm kinder sorry it had to be him.'

Slink Mehaffey grinned, and the greenish scar that curved from his mouth up the left side of his face to his temple made him horrible.

'Guess you ain't puttin' on the weeps fer 'im, tho', eh, Chick?'

'I never cry over spilt blood,' Chick said harshly.

'I got a suit o' clothes that'll fit ye,' Tiny Jo said to Chick.

'An' I kin letcha have a hundred dollars. When you want to pull out?'

'Tomorrow morning,' Chick replied. 'I'm goin' to New York as fast as I can get there without runnin' no crazy chances.'

'You can count on the cops expecting you,' Bledso told him. 'What you'd better do when you get to Jersey is hire a boat and row over to Staten Island, do the same thing from there over Brooklyn, and come in that way. Wait till it's dark and come to my place on Henry Street. I'll give you the directions before you leave here.'

'You're a square guy, Bledso,' Chick said sincerely. 'I won't forget that when things is comin' my way.'

'Barney is reg'lar,' Tiny Jo declared.

Bledso laughed. 'Let's not talk about that, boys,' he said. 'Let's drink up. That's always a good idea, I've found.'

They did drink up, and presently Chick began to think of a lot of things that perhaps he would not have mentioned had not the liquor loosened his tongue and made him a bit self-pitying and sentimental.

After a while he leaned toward Bledso confidentially.

'You know New York pretty good, don'tcha, Bledso?' he inquired.

'I was born and raised there, and it's my permanent address,' said Bledso. 'What's on your mind, Chick?'

'Ever hear tell of a dame by the name o' – Diamond Lil?'

Bledso plucked at his moustache.

'Well, I should say I have. Diamond Lil? Everybody in New York's heard of her by this time, and I've seen her. She's Queen of the Bowery all right, all right. She's Gus Jordan's woman — '

'Gus Jordan's woman!' Chick echoed.

'Yes,' said Bledso. 'He's a ward boss. Going to be next sheriff of New York County. He owns a big saloon and dance-hall on Chatham Square. They call his place Suicide Hall, because it's rumoured that a lot of down-and-outers, both men and women, finished themselves there.'

''Course, she wears a lot o' diamonds, is why they call her Diamond Lil eh?'

'That's right,' Bledso laughed. 'She's got 'em draped all over her. But if you're figuring to get your hands on any of that you might as well save yourself the time. You couldn't get near her to get it. If you tried, you'd be dead and your body on the way to the East River before it was cold.'

'Oh, they's a lot o' tough lugs around protectin' her, eh?' Chick demanded surlily.

'Say, she's got guys around her that'd die for her,' Bledso declared.

'Hum!' Chick grunted. Then muttered to himself: 'She would be the kind to have a regiment around her. The dirty turn-tail!'

'All the society people in New York go down to the Bowery to see Diamond Lil. She entertains every midnight with a song and dance that steams 'em up.'

'Yer say she's gotta whole heap o' diamonds, huh?' Chick wanted to be reassured.

Bledso laughed. 'Say, she's got enough ice to put on a production of *Uncle Tom's Cabin*. Gus Jordan must get her some new rocks after every time he sleeps with her.'

'Cripes!' Chick bounced up out of his chair. 'Don't talk like that. I can't stand it!'

The three men stared at him in amazement. He looked down at them for a moment, blazing with fury, then his face relaxed and he slumped back into the chair he had left so precipitately.

'Sorry, boys!' he said off-hand. 'There was a little matter between me and her once.'

Bledso's beady eyes were fixed on Chick.

'Hm, yes, now I recall something, Chick,' he said. 'All I can say is: Go slow, boy. Go slow.'

Chick's mouth twisted in a nasty grin. 'I'll go slow. Yeah, I'll go slow. But I'll go sure! Sure!' He turned to Tiny Jo. 'You got to fix me up with a shootin'-iron, Tiny. No tellin',' he added, 'when I might have to clip a coupla sparrows to keep from starvin', hey?'

Slink Mehaffey laughed like a damned soul.

'Haw! Yer a card, Chick. Sparrers, be blowed! An' maybe them sparrers'll be wearin' pants an' maybe they'll be wearin' corsets, hey, cull?'

Tiny Jo stopped picking his nose and wiped it with the back of a monstrous hand. 'I'll gitcha a gun, Chick. But don't go to gunnin' nobody in New York. Youse is goin' to be hangin' round the Five Points district, and thim lads is so tough they'd barbecue yer gut for a communion breakfast.'

Chick laughed harshly.

'Say, I ain't no yeller pimp what's scared of his own shadder. I'm goin' to New York fer one reason. I ain't sayin' what. But if I got to plant some lugs under the pussy-willers, to git what I wants, they better start drinkin' holy water right now, 'cause when I starts they ain't goin' to have time to read no Bible.'

'I wouldn't go lookin' for trouble, Chick,' Barney Bledso told him. 'It don't pay.'

Chick snorted.

'Nothin' pays,' he said cynically. 'Not a goddam thing pays. Goin' straight don't pay. Goin' crooked don't pay. Lovin' a woman don't pay! Lovin' God don't pay! Nothin' pays, nothin' pays, nothin' pays! If you're square you're a soft-headed sap! If you're a crosser, you're a yellow bastard! If you go to hell for a woman, you're a easy-mark an' a blasted fool! If you treats a woman like dirt, she puts rat-poison in yer coffee and sends you to hell anyway! Why, what's life good fer, anyhow? The minute you crawl into the world for no good reason of yer own it's got you licked four ways from the ace. What the hell's the difference in the end if I kill forty fat slobs o' cops or spend me life hoein' potatoes?' He was working himself up, the liquor helping him. 'You guys don't know what hell is. You ain't never looked at iron bars day after day. Yer see 'em all day, and you see 'em in yer dreams. Yer see the shadder of 'em in yer cup o' water. Yer see the shadder of 'em acrost yer bread. When yer dreams o' the woman yer left outside, the goddam bars are atween yer. Yer reach out fer her body and it feels like iron. Yer kiss her an' the kiss tastes like iron.' He began to laugh, but his voice came like a sob. 'An' when she's double-crossed yer when she swore to stick till hell froze over! When she's lovin' another guy while you're rottin' in gaol. You want to kill! D'you hear me? You want to shoot the heart out o' every son of a bitch that's kissed her! I said I knew where there was ice I could get my hands on, and I'll get it if it's the last thing I do.' His voice rose to a scream. 'An' if I go to hell for it, I'll have company. But that cheatin' double-crossin' whore'd prob'bly sleep with the devil!'

14

FOR A MAN

DIAMOND LIL'S first meeting with the striking Captain Cummings, and the resulting skirmish of wits in which she had come off apparently the better, since the Salvationist had beat a hasty and unceremonious retreat, left her in a highly unusual state of mind.

Lil did not try to blind herself to the facts. Preacher or no preacher, psalm-singer or what not, she wanted that man more than she had ever wanted any man in her life before.

Her first contact with him had been so sudden, so unprepared for, that her reaction and subsequent high-handed treatment of the captain was an instinctive protest growing out of the feeling that she was inferior, at least morally, to this man who professed Jesus and did the work of God.

She had desired the man from the moment she had seen him conducting the street meeting under her window. Before she had even met him face to face she had felt in her heart that he was too good for her. She did not cherish that thought. She felt, too, that the captain would only look upon her as a bad woman whom he must bring unto salvation, to a realization of the 'Resurrection and the Life'. He would be interested in her only from the angle of redemption. And that was not at all the way in which Lil wanted him to be interested in her.

127

And so she had taken the surest way, if she had only known it, of awakening his interest in her as a woman of flesh and blood rather than as just another soul to be saved, by belittling his good works, by denying his God, whom he served, and by piercing the armour of his righteousness and telling him in her own way that she knew that underneath he was a man with the emotions and fleshly desires of other men; and that he was a fool to look upon beauty and an invitation to voluptuous delights and remain so disregardful of the promptings of his manhood and to refuse the charms she offered him

Lil spent a lot of time thinking it all over. Captain Cummings was going to be hard to get. She realized that, while her inviting him to come up and visit her practically gave him entrée to her gold swan bed, it had only served to stamp her on his mind. She wondered and wondered whether her frankness had not merely scared him off. She wasn't foolish enough to think for a minute that, even if he was not as sincerely religious as she had every right to believe he was, he would cast everything aside and establish the relation with her that she so desired.

She began to argue with herself whether or not it would be better to change her tactics on their next meeting. She was sure there would be a next meeting. Perhaps it would be wise, she told herself, if she let on that she had taken some of his good counsel to heart, and that she was willing to make an effort to tread the straight and narrow. And perhaps, without saying it, she might be able to make him feel that she was doing so because she wanted him to think well of her.

In her whole life she had never been so sincerely moved by a man as she was by the handsome Captain Cummings. She had never met a man just like him, a man who was so utterly clean, and far removed from the temptations of the flesh. She could not bring herself to believe that he had never known the body of a woman. Yet she was almost certain that there could not have been many. Perhaps only one. He would be the type who had given all his love and faith into the keeping of one woman, and then, disillusioned by her, had sought consolation in attempting to save others from destruction.

At one moment she played with the idea of how heavenly it would be to teach him, who must be a novice, the rich varieties of love that experience had taught her. And then, at the next, she saw him as someone totally apart from the world she had known. She recognized in him a nobility of character that ran deeper than mere pretence. Lil was uncultured, but her insight and understanding were keen. At such a moment, down in her heart she felt an impulse, a desire to be raised up to his level.

All this was the strangest development in Lil's gaudy career.

The thing that puzzled Lil, though, was just how to start being good. What made people good? And what was it like to be good? It couldn't be very amusing she thought, or people wouldn't find so much fun in being bad. And just what did a person have to do to be bad?

After all, she argued, the things she had done and was doing didn't hurt anybody. Chick Clark, of course, had gone to gaol for swiping the rocks he had given her. But then, that wasn't her fault. He was a crook before she met him, and he would have stolen the rocks, anyway, even if he hadn't had her to give them to. Sleepin' with a lot of different men might be considered a bit out of order, but then she hadn't hurt them any; hadn't wrecked any homes or anything like that. In fact, she had made them very happy, and she had enjoyed it all too. So what was the harm in skin to skin, if you had a lot of fun and nobody got cut?

It was breaking one of the Ten Commandments. But then, Lil had never liked Moses, and she wasn't quite sure that the old patriarch hadn't chiselled out those ten restrictions on a hunk of rock of his own accord, just because he was feeling a little bilious, and it pained him to see healthy people enjoying themselves.

However, that afternoon, a few days after her *contretemps* with Captain Cummings, she had heard a rumour concerning Jacobsen's Hall and the Salvation Army. There seemed to be some difficulty or other. She had dispatched Frances to learn the details. Now it was early evening, and she was beginning to wonder whether Frances was ever coming back, when the door of her bedroom opened and that very person slid in wearing the complacent smile of a Cheshire cat.

'What the hell took you so long?' Lil demanded with a touch of annoyance. 'I thought you fell down a manhole or somethin'.'

'I had to wait around to see Jacobsen.'

'Oh, he does own the hall?'

'Yeah,' said Frances. 'His first name is Isaac.'

'Very appropriate,' said Lil. 'Did you tell him to come here and see me?'

'Yeah. He said he'd be over in a little while. He said he wanted to put on a clean collar, but I told him you couldn't see it under his beard, anyway. Then he said something in Yiddish that didn't sound good, and he says when a gentleman calls on a lady like Diamond Lil he can't look like a bum.'

Lil laughed 'Maybe he's hopin' I'll seduce him.'

'Oh,' said Frances, 'he's probably comin' over with a truck figurin' he's in line to haul away all yer rocks.'

'Was the Army captain there?' Lil asked casually.

'Not then,' replied Frances, 'but I seen him go in after I left. Say, Lil, you ain't fallin' for this here Salvation guy, are ya?'

Lil reached for a cigarette and avoided Frances's eyes.

'Oh, it ain't nothin' serious,' she said, 'only there was somethin' just wonderful about him.'

Frances shook her head. Lil had often advised her against love, and she felt that now was just the time to return some of that advice.

'That's the way it starts, Lil,' she warned. 'It's just that way that landed me in Chinatown. You're not fallin' for this soul-saver?'

Lil waved her cigarette.

'Why, he wouldn't even look at me, 'cept out o' curiosity.'

Frances looked at her.

'You don't know what he was before he was vaccinated with religion,' she offered.

'Not this one, Frances,' Lil protested. 'He's different.'

Frances couldn't see it.

'Aw, them guys is always different. Does Jordan know you sorter like this Salvationer?'

'Who said I liked him?' Lil snapped. 'I just want to know something about him. Who he is and where he comes from.'

'In plain English, you just want the low-down on this bird?'

'That's it,' Lil agreed.

'I don't think you'll get much outer Jacobsen,' Frances told her. 'Them kind always keeps it behind the ears.'

Lil picked a thread of tobacco from her lips.

'Oh, I don't want to see him for that. You see, I know the Army is kind of poor. I heard they was goin' to be put out . . . and . . .'

'Gawd! You got it bad!' Frances exclaimed. She stared at Lil a moment. Then added: 'You know, Jordan thinks a awful lot of you, Lil!'

Lil turned around. Bringing in Jordan just when she was thinking of the captain irritated her.

'Well, don't I know it?' she retorted. 'Why shouldn't he? Ain't I known from one end of the Bowery to the other as his woman? Jordan's gettin' on in years. I'm doin' him a favour.'

'Jordan's a big map down here,' Frances went on dreamily. 'Many a skirt would think herself a queen if he'd give her a tumble.'

Lil's hand went out expressively.

'Once I get them they're branded,' she declared.

Frances sighed.

131

'Them's the truest words you ever said, Lil. No other woman could hold him.' She paused. 'That boy from Brazil. You know, Rita's friend? Looks to me like he might be a burnin' lover if you ask me. Have you tried him out yet?'

Lil shot her a searching look. Had the janitor told Frances about the use she had made of her room?

'God, no!' she returned with an uneasy laugh. 'But it takes all the time I have to hold him off. And how that boy can kiss – hands, I mean.'

'Well, take a tip from me,' Fances cautioned. 'Keep your eyes on his hip pocket. Them kind o' guys always has a knife handy.'

Lil reflected upon the handiness of Señor Juarez.

A knock on the door interrupted her thoughts.

'See who it is, Frances.'

She crossed to her dressing-table and gave her hair a few touches.

'It's Chuck,' Frances announced.

'Come in, Chuck,' Lil said.

Chuck came in without bothering to remove the hat from his head or the cigar from his mouth.

'Hello, Lil,' Chuck greeted her. 'Say, Ike Jacobsen is outside in de hall. He says he wantsa speak witcha.'

'Tell him to come in,' Lil said.

Without moving, Chuck shouted: 'Hey, Ike. Come in.'

Isaac Jacobsen came in. He was a middle-aged man with an orthodox beard. He must have changed more than his collar, for he wore a dark cutaway coat, white vest and grey-striped trousers all neatly pressed. A diamond sparkled on the little finger of his left hand. But a derby hat was pulled so far down on his head that it made his ears stick out like the handles on a bouillon cup. A stick was crooked over an elbow and he held yellow gloves in his hand.

When he saw Lil he pried the derby off his head.

'Vell, vat can I do for you, Diamond Lillie?' he inquired.

'Sit down,' said Lil. 'I'll be right with you. See you later, Frances.'

Frances took the hint and went out.

Jacobsen was amazed by the luxury of the room.

'My! Vat a fine place you got here!' he exclaimed. He smacked his lips in appreciation.

Chuck didn't want Jacobsen to miss any of the fine points. He was even prouder of that room than Lil was. Chuck liked to talk to Lil there and sit on her gold chairs.

'You betcha life dis is a fine joint,' he told Jacobsen. 'Ain't no oter' like it on de Bow'ry. Look at dis here bed. Know where dat come from?'

'No. Vere?' 'Jacobsen asked, staring at the bed with wide-open eyes.

'Paris,' said Chuck, and his voice held a note of awe. 'And dis wardrobe, and dem fixshers. Cost money, kid. T'ousands.' He paused, catching Lil's eye. 'Want me to breeze, Lil?'

Lil smiled. 'Yeah. Go ahead. I ain't goin' to kiss him.'

Chuck almost swallowed his cigar. 'Wot? Him?' he roared, and went out. Lil could hear him laughing all the way downstairs.

While she talked to Jacobsen she busied herself at her dressing-table.

'I see the Army has rented your building,' she said by way of beginning.

Jacobsen seated himself on the sofa and turned to her. 'Rented it, sure. But dey ain't got no money. So how can I keep dem dere?'

'Ain't goin' to put them out, are you?' Lil inquired casually.

'No-o-o,' drawled the elegant Mr. Jacobsen. 'I'm joost goin' to tell dem to move.'

'Have you told them yet?' Lil wanted to know.

Jacobsen waggled his head.

'Vell, I did mention it to de captain. He tells me to vait – maybe next mont' de collections will be better, so everythink vill be alleright. But I can't take a chence. Money is money. It's true dey are very fine pipple. Movvelous pipple. But everythink dey get dey giff avay.'

Lil wanted to be positive, so she asked:

'Captain Cummings is connected over there?'

Jacobsen nodded.

'Yeh, yeh! A nice, smartish-lookin' feller, but no money. No mazuma.' He rose from the sofa and clasped his hands together. 'Vell, my dear lady, vhy am I here? You vant to sell me some of your diamonds, odder — '

Lil faced him.

'Nope. Now listen, Jacobsen. What will you take for that building where the Army is?'

Jacobsen's mouth fell open in astonishment.

'Now don't start multiplying,' Lil warned him. 'I don't want to buy the Bowery. You know, the best bandit rode a horse.'

Jacobsen smiled suavely.

'A horse or a jack-ass. Vat's de difference? I vas goink to esk tventy-fife t'ousand dollars. It's vort' tventy, but I'll take fifteen.'

'Twelve thousand and like it,' said Lil.

Jacobsen threw up his hands.

'Oi! No, no! I couldn't do dat!' He started for the door, exclaiming in Yiddish that he was insulted; he was being robbed; to his own mother he would not sell it for twelve thousand.

Lil let him get to the door. 'Good-bye, Jacobsen,' she said.

He spun round as though he had been stung.

'Good-bye? No! Vait! Vait! Vait! Is dis all cash? No mortgages goes wit' it?'

'All cash,' said Lil in an off-hand manner, as though she was no longer especially interested.

Jacobsen came back. He had the appearance of a man whose heart had just been broken.

'Vell,' he said hesitatingly. 'It's pretty cheap alle-right, but I'll do it for you, Diamond Lillie.'

'Good,' said Lil briskly. 'Now you get the papers drawn up and make it look as if the Army has bought the building themselves.'

A knock sounded at the door.

'Come in,' Lil called.

Bill poked in his head, his right cheek distorted by a quid of tobacco.

'That Salvation Army man is downstairs,' he said, 'and wants to see you right away.'

'All right,' Lil replied. 'Show him the way up.'

Bill closed the door. Lil talked fast.

'Now, listen, Jacobsen. Don't mention my name to a living soul about this. No one would believe you if you did.'

'If you vant me, I'll be dem and duff,' Jacobsen swore.

'That's the way to be, Jacobsen,' Lil said, casting critical glances at herself in the mirror.

Jacobsen still lingered.

'Diamond Lillie,' he said softly. 'How about a leetle deposit? Dat vould make it binding.'

'Make out a receipt for a hundred dollars,' Lil told him.

'Couldn't you make it two?' he pleaded.

'No, a hundred,' she said firmly. She took one of her photographs from the dressing-table. In it she was gorgeously nude except that she held an ostrich-plume fan in front of her. She handed it to Jacobsen. 'Here, Jacobsen. For the bedroom!'

Isaac gasped.

'Oi! Oi! Oi!' he exclaimed. 'For de bedroom, you say? No, no! I vouldn't even show it to my vife.' He handed her the receipt he had made out and she gave him the hundred dollars. The receipt she hid in the *bonheur du jour*.

Jacobsen took her hand and kissed it. 'Oh, vot a girl! If anybody vas to tell me dat Diamond Lillie ain't got a heart

I vould call dem a dam' liar. Good night, Diamond Lillie. Good night!'

'Good night, Jacobsen, good night!' Lil said hastily. She was adjusting diamond pendants in her ears with all possible speed.

The door closed softly on Jacobsen, and almost immediately afterward she heard Bill's voice directing Captain Cummings.

'Right that way, Captain. That door there on your left. That's it.'

Lil's heart gave a leap. But she quickly picked up a hand mirror and pretended to be very calmly arranging her hair.

She saw the door open, through her mirror, and Captain Cummings came in. Sure, firm, commanding. And his jaw was set in a stern mould.

Lil turned slowly to face him.

15

A CHASTE KISS

'I CAME to inquire the whereabouts of Sally Glynn,' he declared, and there was a trace of impatience in his words. 'I'm told she came here to this place shortly after she had been at the mission. Her father is looking for her. Where is she?'

Lil had been prepared to receive him graciously, but his demand, the import of his words and the tone, at once steeled her and put her on the defensive.

'How should I know?' she said shortly, in answer to his question.

He came towards her, his uniform cap twisting in his hands.

'You know where she is, and I want you to tell me,' he insisted firmly.

Lil looked at him a moment, calculatingly.

'So you come to me to find another woman,' she drawled. 'That's a hot one. Well, I don't know, and I wouldn't tell you if I did.'

The captain's lips tightened aggressively.

'You may get in a great deal of trouble if you do not.'

Lil nodded her head as much as to say: 'I've listened to a lot of hooey like that before.' What she said was:

'So you've come to threaten me? I ain't afraid of you and your whole hymn-squawkin' army.'

Cummings stiffened perceptibly. He felt safe as long as he kept the business of his visit in his mind.

'Why do you take that attitude?' he pursued. 'I came here for information, and I'm going to get it.'

Lil was mildly surprised. No man had ever used that tone to her before. It was an amusing sensation. Her eyes swept over him for an instant; then she lowered her lids.

'I don't know where this Sally is, right now,' she told him. 'And that ain't no lie either.'

The captain relaxed a trifle. His voice became softer.

'I didn't ask you if you knew where she is right now, at this moment. But you know where she was sent, and I want you to tell me.'

Lil wasn't a bit keen for this talk about Sally. Gus had told her that she had got off all right on her trip to South America. That's all she knew. But she had no intention of telling the Salvation Army man even that much.

'Why don't you pray for your answer?' she baited him. 'Why come to a devil like me?'

Cummings felt a strange pang at that. He gave her a pleading look.

'Because I know that somewhere inside of you there must be a heart. Why, the mother of this girl is dying because of her grief at not knowing where she is. Surely you won't hesitate to help me find the girl?'

Lil swaggered nearer to him.

'Well, it's a good story. Not new – but good!'

The blood drained from the captain's face for a moment, and then flooded back again and left it blazing.

'Why, surely . . . ' he stammered. 'You don't mean to infer that I'm lying to you?'

'It has been done,' Lil informed him cynically. She slid past him towards her sofa. 'No. I'm more likely accusin' you of bein' the father of her unborn child.'

He wheeled about on her, fairly shaking.

'How dare you say such a thing to me?' he ground out.

'You're certainly damn' interested,' she replied coolly.

'It's my duty!' he retorted hotly.

Lil's eyes narrowed. 'Humph! Your duty! That's a high-powered word with you people.' She leaned her hands on the back of the sofa. 'Why don't you start tryin' to save people before they need it? It'd be more to your credit.'

'Oh, if only we could!' he said intensely. 'Come, now, do one decent thing in your life. Tell me where this girl was sent?'

He had created an opening. Lil was quick on the uptake.

'You think I *could* do one decent thing?' she asked quietly, and her eyes widened into his with a look that seemed to say: 'If you had faith in me, I could do anything; be anything.'

'Yes,' he said fervently. 'I *know* you could. Come, now, won't you tell me? Please! *Please!*'

Lil was never one to tell tales that might in any way involve Gus, but the look of earnest pleading on the captain's handsome face touched her.

'She went to Rio,' she said, looking away.

'Rio!' he cried. 'Good God!'

'She went of her own free will,' she added. 'She had to get away from these parts for a while. It was necessary.'

'When did she sail?' he demanded quickly. 'Who went with her?'

'She went alone,' Lil replied. She wasn't sure about that, but she wasn't sure either that she hadn't. So she let the statement stand.

'Who paid her passage?' Cummings shot at her.

'Say, if you came here to trick me into something,' she snapped.

He shook his head negatively.

'I'm not trying to implicate you in anything, Lillian,' he assured her.

'Lillian!' Lil exclaimed. It did something to her.

'Lillian is your name, isn't it?' he asked.

That was in a past she rather not remember. It had no connection with the Diamond Lil of the present.

'It's a long time since I was called Lillian,' she replied softly. 'Why don't you call me Diamond Lil, same as all the rest?'

'Because, because,' – his voice shook – 'you're not Diamond Lil to me . . . ' His arms made an involuntary forward movement, then he dropped them quickly to his side and turned away. 'I'm sorry – I must be going.'

There was a flash of lightning and a rumble of thunder. A hot, dusty odour came up through the open window on a sudden gust of pre-storm wind.

'Oh, now that you've got what you want of me,' she said bitingly, 'you're going.'

His cap twisted in his hands as he looked at her.

'What more is there to be said?'

Lil watched him steadily.

'I bet you got a past that could draw rings around this Bowery,' she said.

'If I have, I know nothing of it,' he returned with a certain nervousness.

Lil was not satisfied with that.

'You mean to say you've never made love to any woman?' she asked incredulously.

'I have never been in love with any woman,' he asserted.

'You know what I mean,' she pursued. 'Ain't you never wanted to hold a woman close – very close?'

His eyes were upon her and in them was a strange light. She stood before him a-shimmer with the fire of diamonds, her breasts were a white lure.

'I may have wanted it,' he murmured, 'but – but — '

'You ain't no virgin, are you?'

There was a blinding flash, and thunder rattled the universe. Lil half turned towards the window and drew back

140

against him. For an instant his hands gripped her shoulders protectingly. Then at a sudden realization of the intimacy he dropped his hands. She faced him. He looked down at his hands.

'You see,' he faltered, 'you don't know as much about men as you think you do. We're not all the same. I mean that some men can talk with a woman without – without — '

'Without what?' Lil demanded to know.

'Without wanting to make love to her,' he finished lamely. Her lips moved for a smile, but she checked it.

'I do appeal to you?'

'You might, if I permitted myself to think about it,' he admitted.

'Now,' Lil told herself, 'we're gettin' somewhere.' Lightning ripped across the window and thunder snarled like a cur at its heels. Rain followed wildly, jabbing its wet bayonets into everything. Lil crossed to the window and closed it.

'You can't go out in this,' she told the captain. 'Come over here and sit down and talk to me.' She seated herself comfortably on the sofa.

Hesitatingly, he sat gingerly on the edge of the sofa beside her.

'Have a cigarette?' she offered.

'Thanks, no. I don't smoke.'

Lil smiled genially. 'Yes, I guess before long smoking is goin' to make a man look effeminate like.'

The captain allowed himself the first smile since he had entered the room.

'I'm afraid so,' he said. 'Some women are taking it up, I understand.'

'Of course, you don't approve?' Lil remarked, lighting a cigarette and inhaling deeply.

The captain gave it serious thought.

'It's one of the most harmless of vices. Still, I think it takes away from any woman's natural charm.'

Lil crossed her legs with great obviousness, revealing a goodly portion of the top one. The captain quickly averted his eyes, while she gave him an amused look. This was sport, Lil decided. What an innocent he was! Ripe for teaching.

He saw the glitter of diamonds on her dressing-table. Things she had not put on. He sprang up nervously from the sofa and, going to the dresser, he picked up a handful of the things brooches, pendants, rings. He held them out to her.

'So this is why they call you Diamond Lil?'

'Yeah,' she drawled lazily. 'Ain't they beauties?'

'Exquisite.' He stared at them. 'But aren't you afraid to leave them about so carelessly?'

Lil crushed out her cigarette.

'No one comes in here but folks I know, and they wouldn't touch anything but me.'

'You don't know,' he said earnestly. 'I may be just the one to take both.'

Lil's eyes widened in surprise. Then she laughed.

'You? Why, you ain't got guts enough to pull off anything like that. You'd be afraid of being caught.'

He replaced the diamonds and came towards her.

'You think I'm a coward, do you?' he demanded, and his lips formed into a thin line.

'All you goody-goodies is cowards at heart. That's why you're out to reform folks who's got the nerve to do the things you'd like to do but dare not.'

'That's interesting logic' – with a touch of asperity. 'Then you think no one is good because they want to be?'

Lil waved a hand as much to indicate that it was all cut and dried as far as she was concerned.

'How could they be?' she asked in a manner that hinted that the subject was beginning to bore her. 'No excitement, no adventure. It ain't natural to like that kind of life. They

just kid theirselves that they're havin' a good time. At heart
they're plaster saints, wishin' they had somethin' besides a
wet string up their backs.'

'You think that dodging cops and stealing right and left is
having a good time?' he flared.

'Well, it *is* exciting. Life is a dam' tiresome performance if
you spend it runnin' around in circles like you.

'That may be true,' he, returned, 'but it *is* peaceful!'

'Peaceful!' Lil laughed mockingly. 'You get enough of that
when you're dead.'

'What makes you so sure of that?'

'Because when you're dead, you're dead,' she said
impatiently. 'That's the end of it.'

'I assure you that you're mistaken,' he quickly protested.

This was all getting too metaphysical for Lil. It was
drifting away from the main problem, and that was to get this
apparently timid young fellow in a frame of mind that would
eventually lead him beneath the blankets of the swan bed or
any other that would serve the purpose.

'I ain't going to argue about it,' she declared. 'Because I for
one don't pretend to actually know, I only know I'm here
right now, and I'm going to have all the fun out of life I can.'
She turned her attention to the sparkle of her fingers. She
held them up. 'Aren't they beauties?'

'Dazzling!' he cried. 'You remind me of a glittering palace
of ice.'

'I ain't ice,' Lil assured him.

He looked perplexed for a second.

'I didn't mean to imply that you were,' he said apolo-
getically. 'Diamonds always seem so cold to me. They have
no warmth. No soul.'

'Why, diamonds is the most valuable thing a body could
have,' Lil asserted with conviction.

'The body, yes. But not the soul.'

'Maybe I ain't got no soul,' she retorted.

'Yes, you have,' he said earnestly, 'but you keep it hidden under a mask. But you'll wake up some time.'

A crash of thunder drowned out whatever he might have added. Then he picked up his cap from the sofa where he had placed it and turned to her.

'I've got to be going back to the mission. Sally's father will be waiting for me.'

Lil's eyes were fixed on him. She was thinking that she'd have to take matters into her own hands. She was silent, watching him.

He extended a hand hesitantly.

'Good-bye, Lillian,' he said. She ignored his out-stretched hand as she moved towards him with a seductive languor.

His hand sought the knob of the door and opened it. Her hand pushed it shut. He drew back in surprise. She was close to him now. Her body pressed his. The fragrance of her enveloped him. Her arms, sleek white tentacles, encircling his neck. Her lips were a flaming hibiscus turned up to his. For a moment he held her to him fiercely. Then his lips touched her forehead ever so lightly. He released her and dashed out of the door.

Lil was actually shocked. She gazed at the closed door for several minutes. Had it all been a dream? Finally, she started to laugh.

'To think I'd stand for a kiss like that!' she murmured. 'Well, it won't be long now. No soul! Aw, he would say something like that!'

16

CROWDED HOUR

GUS JORDAN was feeling easier in mind. He had managed to ship off Sally Glynn along with twelve other girls a few days after he had placed her in Charlie Fong's long, yellow, solicitous hands. They had been lucky in getting enough girls to make the shipment to Rio worth while. Gus's share, when they were marketed, would be about six thousand dollars. The Chink would get a thousand for his trouble, and Rita would net about four thousand on the deal.

One can see that Jordan hesitated to drop this line of endeavour, risky as it was, for it was bringing him a handsome income. Four times a year Rita came to New York, and sometimes they bagged as high as thirty pretty birds for the carnal aviaries of the hot countries below the Equator. That was just one consignment of goods. A good year brought Gus from twenty-five to thirty thousand dollars. A man coming up in politics needed money. A man who wanted to keep Diamond Lil in the style to which she had accustomed him had to have even more. The flesh marts of South America had just begun to turn to the northern continent for brothel fodder, and Gus with Rita as his point of contact had got in on the ground floor, so to speak.

Of late, the rather active movement for reform in the city

administration had caused Gus some worry. It had not been any too pleasant to learn that he was being checked up by an agent of the law who could not even be identified, much less corrupted by the usually infallible silencer, hush money.

But now he had little to worry about. Charlie Fong's trap was empty of prey. Although Rita and her – in Gus's opinion – slimy confederate, Juarez, still lingered, the prospective sheriff felt that the world was rather a nice place to live in. He had money, he had preferment, and best of all he had Diamond Lil. What more could a man ask, who wanted nothing to do with God?

In addition to all that, his place was growing more and more crowded every night. Lil had not only brought him love, he told himself; she had brought popularity to his dance hall. Her dazzling presence had turned the tide for him. He was meeting and shaking the hand of persons whom he would never have seen – bluebloods, dandies, the silk-stocking, moneyed crowd whose approbation or disapprobation could make or break a place. Lil had won them all to her. She represented to the snooty bunch, with their extraordinary fads, fancies and purple philosophies, the beauty and daring of sin that was unashamed. In the flavoured words of Chuck: 'Dey took de clo'es-pins offen deir noses when dey come down to see Diamond Lil. Dey was ready fer any'ting. Even a little rape would've went swell.'

It was then, with a great deal of complacence, that Gus surveyed his domain on the evening that the thunderstorm caught Captain Cummings in Lil's bedroom. He stood at his polished bar drinking a whisky-sour, and suddenly remembered that he hadn't seen Lil all day.

Lil hugged to herself the thought that she had stirred up Captain Cummings to an admission of interest in her. An interest that was not alone concerned with the state of her soul. As unsatisfying and meticulously pure as the kiss she had finally won from him had been, yet Lil took it as significant. It was progress, to say the least, along the path she desired to lead the protagonist of salvation

She had half-hour before she needed to commence dressing for the evening. The rain still beat down upon the window and on the shed immediately beneath. The thunder was rumbling far in the distance, and there was only an occasional flash of heat lightning. The worst of it was over.

Lil prepared to lie upon the bed for a brief rest. The dress she had worn that day she picked up from where she had carelessly left it on a chair and carried it to the wardrobe and hung it within. Then she turned out the lights, save for one dim jet burning on a bracket near her dressing-table. As she moved towards her bed a sound behind her made her turn her head quickly. Her window-sash was being raised. She swung round and faced it. A dark form stepped through the aperture and shed streams of water upon the floor. As thin rays of the single gas-jet fell upon the unshaven face of the intruder who was shaking the water from a black felt hat, Lil cried out.

'Chick!' Her exclamation was guarded despite her surprise. Which perhaps wasn't so much surprise after all. She drew away from the man who came toward her, clearly menacing.

'You don't seem very glad to see me,' he sneered, coming close to her so that his face was only a few inches from hers.

'I can't say I am,' she returned quickly. 'How'd you know how to get in?'

'I was tipped off at Kelly's how to get to you. That shed under the window.'

'Bein' in gaol ain't made you ferget none o' your second-story work,' she jeered.

They were startled to hear Jordan's voice dangerously near. It seemed so, at any rate. He was calling for Bill to come to him. Lil locked the door.

'I been layin' low waitin' for a chance to get to you,' Chick said. 'The storm gimme a break and here I am.'

'What do you want here?' Lil demanded none too pleasantly.

Chick's lips twisted in a snarl.

'Not much like the dame 'at clung to me a few months back and said she'd stick till Hell froze over.'

'Wha'ja expect me to do?' Lil snapped. 'Enter a convent?'

'I went to the pen for you,' he told her through clenched teeth.

'For me?' Lil cried derisively. 'Say, you was flirtin' with the State's hotel long before I ever met you.'

Chick's lower lip stuck out in an ugly leer.

'I see you're wearing some o' them rocks I got in the deal I was sent up for.'

'Say, what do you want here, anyway?' she impatiently demanded. She felt no fear of him.

Again he came closer to her.

'I want you to pack up and go to Paris with me.'

Lil all but laughed in his stricken face.

'Say, do you think I'd be fool enough to go any place with you?'

'You mean you won't go with me?' he rasped.

'Of course not!' she replied coolly.

'I was good to you back in Chicago,' he reminded her, his eyes points of steel daggers. 'Too damn' good! An' after I got the works, night after night I laid thinkin' about you. My one aim was to get out an' get to you. Even when I did make the break and got here, to learn that you was Jordan's woman . . . Still, I reasoned if I could get back to you you'd go with me. We could start over together. I'd be willin' to forget you crossed me.'

Lil turned away and passed to the other side of the bed. He followed her.

'Well, I ain't goin', Chick,' she said. 'I'm staying here.'

'Don't you love me any more?' he pleaded.

'Any more?' Lil echoed.

His voice flew up.

'You mean to say you never loved me?'

'Why, women don't love your kind of men,' she said flatly.

'Damn you!' he cried, raising his knotted fists. 'I'll – I'll — '

'You'll what?' Lil retorted. 'Say, all I gotta do is call Jordan and your trip will be back to Chicago.'

His face suffused with bloody rage.

'You'll never live to see me go.'

'None of them cheap threats,' she warned him. 'You ought to know me better than to try that stuff on me.'

'Why, you're lower than a whore on this here Bowery,' he said viciously. 'She don't pretend somethin' she don't feel. You don't love this Jordan, do you?'

'Don't be a fool,' Lil answered.

'Don't be a fool?' he repeated. 'That's just what I am. A rotten fool for you. Jumpin' freights. No sleep for days. Crawlin' through the mud to get to you. Am I a man or a louse to let you do this to me?'

'What do you want, money?' Lil inquired sharply.

'No, I don't want money,' Chick ground out. 'If did, I know where to get it.'

'I tell you, Chick, you're through,' she said with finality.

He caught his breath. Then murder burned red in his eyes. His words were like a steel saw grating across the bars of a cell-window.

'So you're through? Very pretty, *Diamond* Lil. But *I'm* not through. You think you're gonna lay your skin with other guys after the chances I took to get to you? You're goin' with me now, I'll tell you.'

Lil's voice came like a whip.

'I'm tellin' you to get out! You're through!'

'Damn your soul to hell!' he ripped out 'You got the nerve to stand there and tell me to get out! Why, you — ' His hands gripped her throat and flung her back upon the bed.

Lil felt as though the life was being squeezed out of her as you squeeze the water out of a washed stocking. Little lights began to dance before her eyes. She tried to scream: 'Gus! Gus!' But the words were no more than a whisper. Was she going to die? Was she really going to die? Her diamonds! Her diamonds! Who would be wearing her diamonds? She couldn't die and leave her diamonds. That couldn't be! That mustn't be! A thousand diamonds sparkled before her eyes. They whirled around in a pin-wheel. Far off she heard a voice crying: 'Cheat! Welsher! Double-crosser! Whore!' Then darkness settled round her. Suddenly she heard the blows of a sledge-hammer. It was her heart pounding, pounding, forcing her back to life. She opened her eyes. Her body was almost nude and Chick was covering her with hot, hungry kisses.

'Lil! Lil!' he was almost sobbing. 'I couldn't do it! You know I couldn't do it! Don't you know what I feel for you? Ain't you got a heart left in you for me?' All the while his lips moved across her throbbing flesh. 'I love you! I love you, Lil! God, how much I love you! I must have you!'

His lips brushed the roseate buds of her breasts, and an exquisite current passed through her body. She lay still, and Chick Clark did all that a man might be expected to who had hungered and thirsted and suffered for the woman he loved. Something of his old fierce charm possessed Lil, and she could not deny him. Suddenly before the fires of passion could be quenched, they were interrupted by Jordan's voice immediately outside the door of the bedroom.

Chick sprang up with a muffled cry and whipped a revolver from his pocket. Lil rose quickly, too, and drawing her négligé about her, stayed his hand.

'Don't be a fool, Chick!' she whispered. 'You can't get away with anything like that. Go, for God's sake, go!'

Chick pocketed the gun and, seizing her once more in his arms, kissed her. Lil did not restrain him.

'I love you. I'll always love you, Lil,' he whispered hoarsely. 'Remember the good times we had together. Don't back out on me now. Stick like you said you would.'

'I'll meet you at Kelly's tonight, after my turn,' she promised.

'You'll come to me?' Chick wanted to be assured.

'I swear it,' Lil replied.

'I'll be waiting for you,' he said.

A knock sounded at the door, and immediately afterwards Jordan's voice was heard telling someone: 'Let me know when he comes in. I want to see him.'

Chick snatched up his hat and departed through the window. Lil quickly crossed to it and eased down the sash. Then she rapidly lit the other jets, straightened her hair before the mirror, and, drawing a deep breath, went to the door and unlocked it.

It was Frances. Lil emitted a gasp of relief.

'Oh it's you! I thought it was Gus,' she said.

Her face was clouded and her mind preoccupied with the new complications. Chick being in town certainly made a nice mess of everything.

'I thought you might like me to help you dress, Lil,' Frances offered.

'Dress?' said Lil absently. 'Oh yes, dress. I must dress.'

'Which dress are you going to wear tonight?' Frances inquired, opening the wardrobe.

'Which one?' Lil pondered. She tried to jerk her mind back to the business in hand. 'Let me see. Which one? Oh, I don't know. Any one. That one.' She indicated a black gown embroidered with jet sequins.

Frances helped her with her corset, drawing it tight and fastening it. Lil drew on the gown. She fidgeted about as Frances hooked the back of it.

'Are yer nervous, Lil?' Frances asked, having difficulty in fastening the dress with Lil moving about.

'No,' Lil said. Still she continued to fuss.

'Yer are nervous, ain't yer, Lil?' Frances insisted.

'No, no,' said Lil impatiently, and immediately began fumbling with the front of her gown.

That was too much for Frances.

'Are you *sure* you ain't nervous, Lil?'

'No, I ain't *nervous*!' Lil snapped. 'But if you keep askin' me, I will be.'

'I didn't mean to ask yer,' Frances excused herself.

Lil flared. 'Then what the hell are you askin' me for?'

The door was pushed open and Jordan came in ponderously. He shot Lil a quizzical glance.

'Hello, Lil. I ain't seen you all day. Where you been?'

'Frances and the girls was here for a little while, and then this awful storm broke.'

Frances hurriedly fastened the remaining hook and departed.

'Any other visitors?' Gus inquired in a tone that was somehow flat.

Lil hesitated for a bare second.

'Why, that captain from the Army was here.'

'Yeah?' Gus said, looking up suddenly. 'What'd he want?'

'He asked a lot of questions about that Sally Rita sent down to Rio.'

'Hmm! I wonder what for.'

'He said she'd been to the mission that day before she came here. Told a long sad story. Now he says her mother is dyin' and her father is after the Army to try and locate her.'

'What did you say?' Jordan wanted to know.

'I said that she'd gone to Rio of her own free will. Nothin' more.'

Gus stroked his beard with thick fingers.

'Think he believed it?' he asked.

'Yes, I do,' Lil rejoined. 'Them birds is so filled up with religion they can't dope out regular English.'

'Maybe so,' admitted Jordan. 'How long was he here?'

'About half hour,' she replied.

'Half hour!' Gus exclaimed.

'Well,' said Lil petulantly, 'the storm broke and he waited till it was over.'

'Anyone else been here?' he questioned.

'No,' she said.

'You ain't seen that young Juarez?'

'No, course not.'

Jordan sighed and sat down heavily in Lil's armchair.

Lil watched him for a moment.

'Why so funny actin', Gus?' she inquired.

'Funny actin'?' he protested, but only half-heartedly. 'Why, what do you mean?'

'Well,' said Lil, 'you act kinder funny. Have I done anything you don't like?'

'No, no,' he said quickly, and then revealed his thoughts. 'But I tell you, Lil, I don't like this bird Juarez. He's too slimy. Too greasy. Too damn polite to suit me. Why, it ain't natural for a man to be so damn' polite.'

Lil laughed. 'Oh, so that's what's bitin' you.' She came behind his chair and put her arms around his neck. Stroked his hair. 'Why, Gus, he don't mean nothing at all to me. Why, he's Rita's friend, and I thought it was up to me to make him feel good.' She kissed the top of his head.

'I guess I'm a jealous old fool,' he said, taking one of her hands and kissing it. 'But, Lil, I'd kill the man who'd try to get you away from me.'

'Aw, who's tryin'?' Lil replied with a laugh meant to reassure him. She saw that he was looking at her hand which he held. The diamonds made a veritable rainbow of dancing lights. 'They are valuable, ain't they, Gus?'

'Worth damn' near a half million,' he said proudly.

'And he said they had no soul,' Lil murmured half to herself.

'Who said?' Gus demanded quickly.

'That – Army captain,' Lil replied, drawing away from him.

Gus grinned sardonically.

'So you met one guy who won't fall for you, eh?'

'Who wants him to fall?' Lil derided. 'He's the kind a woman'd have to marry to get rid of.'

'Don't be like that, Lil,' Gus said. 'He's got a big job. Don't try to tempt him away from it.'

'I won't. Don't worry,' Lil lied smoothly. 'Although I will admit it would be a satisfaction to see how he'd act.'

Jordan rose. 'Phew! It's stifling in here. Why not open the window?'

'Just what I was going to do, Gus.'

He moved to the window and flung it open. The rain had ceased. He thrust out his head and caught the uprush of sweet rain-washed air.

'Looks like the storm's all over,' he said.

Lil stood petrified in the centre of the room. Her eyes were on the door, which was opening, and she saw that Juarez stood there. Before she could stop him he had entered and was crossing to her with arms out-stretched. Jordan wheeled about and stared momentarily in amazement. Then he let out a roar like a bull.

'So! Damn funny you comin' in here like that without knockin'! What's the meaning of this? How dare you come into this room without knockin'? Answer me!'

Juarez gasped. He hadn't seen Jordan by the window when he entered. He moistened his lips.

'I merely come to pay a visit,' he said lamely. 'A friendly visit.'

'That's no explanation,' Jordan bellowed. 'Lil, what does this mean?'

'Why ask me?' Lil retorted. 'I ain't up on Spanish etiquette. Maybe it's the way they do things down there.'

'Well, it's damn' funny to me.' He snapped at Juarez: 'How often have you made these friendly visits?'

'He ain't never been here before,' Lil cut in.

'Then how'd he know where to come?' Gus demanded harshly.

Juarez waved his hands expressively.

'The waitair, he tell me where.'

'Oh, he did? Let you come up all by yourself, eh?' Gus said sarcastically.

'I theenk I am quite alone,' Juarez replied lightly.

'Yeah! Sure! Now you listen to me. I don't like you and you may as well know it. And what's more, I don't like you hangin' around my place. If Rita wants to be bothered with you, that's her business. Why in hell any woman wants a half-breed is beyond me!'

'Gus!' Lil protested.

'That is quite an insult, Mr. Jordan,' Juarez rebuked him sharply.

'Maybe it is, and maybe I know it,' Gus shouted. 'I don't waste words when I've got anything to say!' He snapped a cigar out of his pocket and bit into it viciously.

'Because my skin is dark is no reason for you to make such a remark!' Juarez flared.

'Well, it's nothin' in your favour,' Gus barked.

'There you go, makin' a mountain out of a molehill,' Lil told Gus. 'Just because he ain't got a brass band to herald his approach, you go off the handle. Here, sit down, Mr. Juarez. You'll have to excuse Gus, he's off key today.'

'That ees quite all right,' said Juarez suavely, seating himself on Lil's sofa. 'I am sorry I have disturb' him.'

'The next time you come up,' warned Lil, 'bring a fife and drum. Will that do you, Gus?'

'I'd rather have him stay out of here altogether,' Gus snarled.

'Now, Gus,' Lil chided. 'You don't mean that. It ain't bein' sociable.'

There came an imperative rapping on the door. Gus opened it. It was Bill.

'Hey Boss,' he said in obvious agitation, 'they're breakin' up downstairs.' The sounds that crashed over his shoulders seemed to indicate that he was telling the truth.

'All right, I'm comin',' Gus said, and Bill disappeared.

Jordan turned to the Brazilian with a hard look. 'See that you're not here when I get back,' he counselled, and went out, slamming the door.

17

LIL TURNS HAIRDRESSER

JORDAN had no sooner gone than Juarez sprang from the sofa and, crossing swiftly to the door, secured it. He had no intention of being caught red-handed again.

Lil laughed at his precaution.

'Gus can be rambunctious when he wants to be,' she told the Brazilian.

Pablo wasted no time. He was over to Lil and had her in his arms in a flash.

'Oh,' he moaned, 'I 'ave miss' you so I can 'ardly stay away!'

'Why did you?' Lil inquired.

'Rita, she ees ver' jealous and has ver' bad temper,' he said with his lips close to her ear. 'I do not want her to fight weeth you.'

'How'd you get loose tonight?' Lil wanted to know.

'She 'ave gone some place weeth Mr. Flynn,' he said, pressing his lips to her shoulder and tightening his hands on her.

Lil pricked up her ears.

'Flynn!' she exclaimed. 'I didn't know that he was interested in Rita.'

'Of much interest,' Juarez murmured in an off-hand way. 'They 'ave many secrets between them.'

'What kind of secrets?' Lil demanded. Many things she had heard about Flynn; things Spider Kane had said began to work in her mind.

'I do not know. I not ask. I love only you,' he said intensely. 'What difference does it make about Rita?'

'Do you suppose she's telling Flynn anything about Jordan's business?' she asked in a more casual tone.

'Perhaps; maybe. What of it?' he inquired in surprise.

She drew away from Juarez.

'If I thought that she'd pull a stunt like that,' she flared, 'I'd – I'd — '

'Don't get excited, sweetheart,' Juarez soothed. 'If anyone harm you I fix him good. Come, forget about Flynn; about Rita. We shall play at love, like that day, hey? Oh, but a minute!' His hand delved into the breast pocket of his coat and returned with a plush box. He opened it, took out a large diamond brooch and tossed the box on the floor. 'Look! I bring you a gift. Diamonds! More diamonds. I know you love them so!'

Lil's eyes glowed with pleasure as he fastened the brooch on the bosom of her gown while she faced the mirror. The stones caught the lights and sent out a fine spray of colours.

'Ain't they grand?' Lil cried. 'Ain't they grand?'

He seized her in a fierce embrace.

'You are beautiful!' he raved. 'See, they make your eyes to sparkle and your teeth to gleam like pearls. Oh, how I love you!' He bent her in his arms and commenced feverishly kissing her breast.

The door they both had thought locked opened violently and closed.

'So!' shrieked Rita. 'This is where I find you!'

Juarez sprang away from Lil.

'Oh, hello, Rita,' Lil greeted calmly. 'I must remember to have that lock fixed.'

'Don't "hello" me!' cried the Latin woman, her eyes blazing.

She turned on Juarez. 'So! The minute my back is turned I find you making love to another woman!'

'What did you expect he'd be doing?' Lil remarked. 'A boy with a gift like that should be workin' at it.'

Rita did her best to ignore Lil. She started again on Juarez, who looked nervous as a young colt.

'What have you got to say for yourself?' she demanded. 'Well – out with it!'

'I have nothing to say,' Juarez admitted weakly. 'You saw. What can I say?'

'You dog! You swine!' Rita flamed. 'How dare you insult me, when I pay for the very clothes on your back!'

'Gawd!' protested Lil. 'You got to give a man more than clothes.'

Rita wheeled on her. 'I'll attend to you later.' She moved close to Juarez and her voice took on a softer note. 'Have you no apology? Are you not sorry? Do you not wish me to forgive you?'

It was Juarez's turn to burn the end of the triangle.

'You were out weeth Mr. Flynn!' he hurled at her. 'How do I know what you were doing?'

Rita stiffened. 'My business with Mr. Flynn was just business, and you know it.' She turned to Lil. 'And now, we shall see!'

'What d'you mean by that?' Lil demanded truculently. She began to suspect that revelations were about to come.

'You'll find out soon enough,' Rita sneered.

'That has all the earmarks of a double-cross to me,' Lil said sharply. 'What do you and this here Flynn think you're pullin' off, anyway?'

'Business,' Rita hissed. 'Pablo knows.'

'Knows what?' Lil snapped.

'I can no tell you, babee,' said Juarez.

'Babee!' cried Rita with indrawn breath. 'So it has gone that far, hey? I go to get Gus Jordan.'

She made as if to go to the door.

'Wait a minute,' warned Lil. 'If anyone here is going to call Gus it'll be me.'

Rita appeared to catch some inference in Lil's words.

'Oh, of course, it is not necessary to call him,' she said affectedly. 'He has nothing to do with it. Perhaps I have been hasty.'

'Hasty?' Lil jeered. 'You've been rapid. But I think you said enough to put me wise to your little game. What do you and this here Flynn think you're doing? Take it from me, Gus will get the both of you.'

'Oh, yes, yes, of course,' Rita mocked. Then suddenly, with an exclamation, her hand shot out and touched the brooch on Lil's gown. 'Where did you get this?'

Lil knocked her hand away. 'None of your damn business!'

Rita flew at Juarez.

'So! You give it to her, you filthy black — ' She broke off and turned again to Lil with a leer. 'So you theenk he has fallen for you, eh, because all men do? I tell you something that will take the feather out of your cap!'

'Do not believe it!' cried Juarez excitedly. 'I swear it is not true!'

'It is true!' Rita spat out. 'You theenk maybe Pablo love you, eh? Well, I tell you Pablo has been paid to make love to you. Mr. Flynn pay him good sum for the job.'

'Flynn?' cried Lil, not knowing whether to believe Rita or not.

Rita laughed harshly.

'Yes. Pablo promised to get certain written documents from you against Jordan.'

'But I did not know you when I make that promise,' Juarez protested in anguish. 'And I have never mentioned anything of him to you, have I?' He crossed to Lil's side. 'Oh, I love you! I swear it!'

Rita's cackle cut across his words like a knife.

'You love her? Maybe she will support you. Oh yes! She

would not buy a man a loaf of bread. She loves only money and diamonds. Her kind don't have no love for men. I bet that when Gus Jordan loses everything he has she laugh and forget him as quick as she did Chick Clark.'

'What do you know about Chick Clark?' Lil shot at her.

'That strike your chest, eh? Well, Chick Clark is right here in New York, and if he once sees you he will kill you, maybe Jordan too.' Then she added with all the venom she could command: 'From what I hear, you lived with Chick Clark in Chicago.'

Juarez directed a stream of Spanish invective at Rita that must have made Satan bank his fires.

'You get out of here and leave her to me,' Lil told him.

Pablo hesitated for a moment and then, giving Rita a black look, slowly went out, closing the door behind him.

Downstairs Ragtime Kelly was caressing the keys sentimentally in the sensuous strains of 'El Choclo'. Its slow beat reached to Lil's room above, but neither woman was conscious of it.

Lil's hand moved to her hips, and the eyes that looked out of her beautiful face at the foreign woman were hard and cold as steel.

'What d'you mean by bustin' in here and insultin' me?' Lil demanded sharply.

'What do you mean by taking my pin?' Rita retorted, indicating the diamond brooch Juarez had presented to Lil.

'I didn't take it; he gave it to me.'

'Well,' said Rita heatedly, 'I want it back, right now!'

What polish Lil ever had was gone now.

'You try and get it!' she said out of the corner of her mouth. 'I wouldn't give you this thing for spite now. If you had asked me for it in the right way you could have had it. I got all the rocks I want' – which was not quite true – 'but I'll keep this here thing to remember you by.'

'Humph!' Rita sniffed. 'You are very clever, Diamond Lil –

so smart, so wise.' Lil turned her back on the Latin woman and busied herself at her dressing-table. In the mirror she saw the expression on Rita's face change from a supercilious sneer to a look of black, murderous hate. She saw the woman fumble with her skirt, the long, black silk stocking, the garter, and then a flash of bright steel.

'In my country we know how to deal with you wise ones!' Rita shrieked. The stiletto gleamed in her hand as she flung herself at Lil. Lil with a gasp wheeled about and was in time to catch the deadly hand. One good thing Chick Clark had done for her – he had playfully taught her a few ju-jutsu tricks that stood her in good stead now. She caught Rita's knife-hand in a grip that forced her arm into a position in which Lil could easily break it with one quick twist.

'Let go my hand! You are hurting me!' Rita cried. 'Oh, oh, oh!' came in a long moan, as Lil forced her back into a chair. Rita's long black hair came undone and cascaded down her back. With a sudden jerk Lil had the stiletto reversed and its keen, needle-like blade was at Rita's heart. Hardly knowing what she was doing, Lil pushed! With a gasping cry Rita's eyes rolled back until only the whites showed. Her body lurched upwards in the chair, convulsed once or twice, and became limp.

'You sneakin', underhanded bitch!' Lil hissed through her clenched teeth. She had retained the blade, and now, looking at it, she saw that it was dyed red with blood. A wild amazement caught her up, 'Help me!' she exclaimed softly, and threw the knife from her. It passed out of sight beneath the wardrobe. What had she done? *What had she done?* She hadn't meant to do it! Her hand just slipped! Things happen that way! 'Rita!' She shook the dead body. 'Rita! Why don't you speak to me?' She moistened her lips, which had suddenly become as dry as tinder. 'Rita! My God!' A dark red sticky stain was gradually growing wider and wider on the bosom of Rita's dress.

Jordan's voice struck her horrified brain like a thunder-clap. 'Oh, Lil! Lil!' She forced her benumbed legs into action and flew to the door and locked it. She turned and stared at Rita, and then the light captured the glitter of the brooch and reflected it in the mirror. She plucked it off her dress and thrust it quickly down inside Rita's dress-front.

'Here, take the damn thing!' Lil cried breathlessly. 'It ain't got no soul, anyway!' She hardly knew what she was saying.

There was a knock at the door.

'Oh, Lil,' came Jordan's voice. Then to someone else: 'I haven't seen anyone. That's funny!'

Lil's hands clenched together so that the nails cut her palms. Her nerves goaded her till she wanted to scream, but with a superhuman effort she mastered the almost overwhelming desire. Quickly her mind clicked and she saw a chance.

She bent over Rita and drew the thick, black mass of Rita's hair over the dead face, so that it was completely hidden. Then she unlocked the door and admitted Jordan and Officer Doheny.

'He must have come up over the shed,' said Doheny, and going to the window thrust out his head and peered around.

'Lil,' said Jordan, 'did you see anyone out there on the shed?'

Lil crossed leisurely to her dresser before replying and picked up a comb and brush.

'No,' she said, with no trace of emotion. 'No.'

'Well, that's funny,' Doheny said. 'He must've made his getaway.' He went out rapidly and down the stairs.

Lil grasped the end of Rita's hair and began gently to run the comb through it from the crown downward, continuing to cover the face.

'What's the matter, Lil?' inquired Gus, not recognizing his former partner. 'We're waiting for you.'

'I'll be right down, Gus,' replied Lil casually. 'I'm just doing a job I never done before. . . '

18

SHADOWS

LIL stared vacantly for a long minute after Jordan had
gone downstairs. There, in one of her best gold chairs,
was a dead woman. It wasn't a dream; it was a ghastly
reality. She had killed Rita. And now what had been Rita was
just as much of a nuisance, only more horrible, as her living
presence had been. There was no escaping going downstairs
and doing her turn. Any protest would arouse suspicion of
something wrong in Jordan and an investigation would reveal
the terrible truth. While impossible thoughts ran through her
mind Lil mechanically prepared herself for her turn in
the dance hall. She hadn't meant to kill Rita, she told herself
over and over. In her heart there was no particular remorse,
however, for the deed, except that by having committed it she
had placed herself in a most awful predicament – dangerous,
but not necessarily a thing to put her in fear of the law. Even
if Gus found out he would not turn her over to the police.
Murder and suicide were not unfamiliar things around the
Bowery; no, not even in Jordan's place. But if he did find out
there would be most disagreeable complications that would
destroy the rhythm and harmony of her existence. It was bad
enough that Chick Clark was in town without this happening.

She must get rid of Rita's body. She couldn't do it herself,
that was one sure thing. Who could she really trust to do the

ugly job? She had no time to attempt anything herself. She dreaded leaving the thing where it was, but she had no alternative.

She went out of the room, locking the door after her. Then as she descended the stairs amidst the applause of the crowd a welcoming smile on her face, her secret fear was that the lock wouldn't hold if someone attempted to enter the room. Then the gig would be up for sure.

How she hated doing the things that night which had always been a pleasure to her . . . receiving the plaudits of the crowd . . . meeting the swells! . . . 'How d'you do; Mrs. Vandermore? Having a good time? . . . Hello Mr. Astervelt, glad you came down? Glad you liked the new number. . . You want "Frankie and Johnny"? All right, I can stand anything if you can.' And all the time Rita was sitting upstairs with her hair blotting out her face. She was stiff by now. She'd be hard to move. While Lil was doing her dance her eyes wandered up to the ceiling. Horrid thought! Suppose the blood should soak through the ceiling and drip, drip, drip! She looked at Mr. Astervelt. Suppose a blob of red suddenly landed on the starched white bosom of his dress shirt? Wouldn't he be surprised? Rita's brothel blood staining the blue-blooded and immaculate Mr. Astervelt. Lil felt a foolish desire to laugh. A few minutes before he had taken the hand of a murderess. He had paid her compliments. Mrs. Vandermore had said in a hushed voice that she didn't believe all the naughty things she had heard about Lil. She told Lil she thought her sweet. Lil had told her: 'Don't go tellin' people that; they won't come here to see me no more. You wouldn't come yourself if you really believed I was a good girl with a bad reputation.' Mrs Vandermore laughingly protested.

At last Lil got away from the crowd that wanted her to be present every minute. She told Gus she was not feeling well and had a splitting headache, which for once was absolutely true. She went to her room; tried the door without inserting the key. It opened for her. A chill swept over her. Had anyone been in while she was downstairs? She looked across at the chair and almost staggered. It was empty! Rita had vanished. Her mind whirled! She caught hold of the back of the sofa and steadied herself.

'Rita gone! Rita gone!' she murmured. Furiously her brain grasped at straws. Had Rita just been feigning, and merely been slightly wounded? A huge wine-coloured stain marked the upholstery of the chair and the rug in front of it. No. Rita had been stone dead. She was sure of it.

She looked closely at the floor and then she saw a little uneven trail of dark spots that had dried and stiffened the nap of the rug. They led to the door. Cautiously she opened it. The trail led on down the short hall; down the stairs that led to a door opening into the alley. Who had done the job? A friend, at least, she reasoned. Anyone else would have raised a holy how. But who? Not knowing worried her. At any rate, she was rid of the corpse, and that was something. She dreaded the idea of sleeping in the room that night.

She had promised to meet Chick Clark. But she was tired now, and lying on the gold swan bed sleep soon obliterated even the memory of Rita, who only a few hours before had quit this life to become madame of some ethereal brothel where space curves voluptuously before Eternity's sweeping face. . .

It was afternoon before Lil descended into the dance-hall next day. Once more the mystery of Rita's disappearance plagued her, and she was in a mood of depression. An extraordinary thing for Lil.

The dance-hall was deserted except for Frances, who was idling at one of the tables over a short beer.

'Hello, Lil!' Frances greeted her.

'Hello, Frances,' Lil returned listlessly, and after a glance into the bar, where two customers were ragging each other, she sat down at the table with Frances.

'Say, Lil,' cried Frances, glowing with the enthusiasm that always prefaced her telling of a piece of news, 'the Salvation Army ain't going to be ditched out of Jacobsen's after all. Somebody bought the joint. Got big-hearted and gave it to them. Ain't it great the way them people get by?'

'Deservin' people just bound to get by,' Lil said, almost with a tremor in her voice. 'I never felt that way before.'

Frances's eyes widened in surprise.

'Jeez, Lil, you talk like you was havin' a attack of religion!'

'No!' said Lil with unnecessary sharpness.

'You ain't in very good humour, are you, Lil?' Frances suggested.

'I'm all right,' Lil replied.

Frances touched her on the shoulder affectionately, and rising from the table went out into the street. She had just gone when Spider Kane, who, unnoticed, had for some minutes past been watching them over the tops of the swinging doors to the bar, came in and crossed quickly to Lil. She looked up questioningly, but he pulled up a chair and sat down before speaking.

'Say, Lil,' Kane began, 'they got a new dick in this precinct. A guy they call "The Hawk". He's the wisest bull in the business. Never lost a man yet. They say he's spottin' this joint day and night.'

Lil's interest was awakened. She thought of Chick.

'Who d'you suppose he's after?'

'I don't know,' responded Kane, 'but there's something goin' on about these here girls Jordan sends down to Rio.'

'What d'you mean, Kane?' Lil queried. 'Why, I seen girls on their knees beggin' for a chance to go down.'

Kane shook his head.

'That's because they didn't know they was goin' straight to hell.'

Lil gave him a level glance.

'Sportin' houses?' she asked.

'Sure, Lil,' said Kane. 'Didn't you know that?'

'To tell you the truth, I never thought much about it, Kane. I never figured Gus for anythin' like that.'

'What d'you think Rita came up here for four times a year? She was a procurer, nothin' else.'

Lil shot him a startled look.

'You said Rita *was*, Kane. What d'you mean by that?'

His eyes lowered to the smeary table.

'I took care of everythin', Lil. Nothin' more's got to be said.'

Lil stared at him in silence for a moment, then she placed a hand on his.

'Thanks, Kane. I only give her what was comin' to her. Rita was nothin' but a — '

'Heavens! Don't mention her!' Kane said quickly.

'Why,' said Lil in surprise, 'I thought you was strong and hardened to them kind of things.'

'I know, but this hit me hard. I can see her yet, like when I t'rew her in the river. Her face turned up and she seemed to laugh at me.'

A chill chased along Lil's spine. But she said:

'Aw, forget it. Everyone will think she went back to Rio. Anyway, if I didn't get her, she'd have got me. Who'd you rather see down there, her or me?'

'Don't say that, Lil,' Kane said with a touch of emotion that seemed out of place in his rough character. 'You know what I think of you. I'm glad I was able to do it for you.'

'How'd you know there was trouble up there?'

'I just felt there was somethin' wrong. And last night when I got a tip that Clark was comin' to get you, and when I heard Jordan call you to sing your songs and you didn't come down, the feelin' got stronger, and so, when I got the chance, up I went. When I seen that moll sittin' there dead, and the hair streamin' down her face – see! That was tough.'

The door of Jordan's office opened and that personage came in. He looked at Kane, who immediately rose and stood uncertainly by the table.

'Ain't worried about anything, are you, Lil?' Jordan inquired.

'Me, worried?' she laughed, but it was forced. 'You ought to know me better than that. What have I to worry about? Say, Kane, have you seen Flynn around anywhere?'

'I left him across at Callahan's,' he said.

'Send him over,' Lil told him. 'I want to see him.'

'I'll do that, Lil,' Kane replied and went out.

Gus lighted a fresh cigar and passed behind Lil's chair.

'Rita ain't shown in today. Have you seen her?' he asked.

Lil hesitated barely the fraction of a second.

'She got sore last night because Juarez gave me a diamond pin. I ain't seen her since.'

'Well, I guess she'll be in before long.'

'If she does it'll be a miracle,' Lil said under her breath.

Jordan turned to her.

'There ain't nothin' between you and this here Juarez, is there, Lil?' he demanded, his eyes watching her shrewdly.

'What! Me take her leavings!' Lil derided. 'I should say not!'

Gus rubbed his beard for a moment and then said:

'Now, I ain't never questioned you like this, as much as you carried on. I believe in giving a woman an open country and she'll generally run straight, but this here Juarez; I never thought he'd part with anything for nothing.'

Lil did not deign to reply. Instead she inquired:

'Gus, have you head anything about this guy they call "The Hawk"?'

His brows contracted and a certain anxious look came into his face.

'No, have you?'

'Kane says he's spotting this place day and night. I think

this here Flynn is back of it all. Flynn ain't no friend of yours, Gus. You might as well know it.'

Gus laughed uncomfortably.

'Why, Flynn and I were boys together. What makes you think that about Flynn?'

Lil looked up at him for the first time since he had come in.

'He's jealous of you. Everyone knows he would love to be boss of this here district.'

Gus grunted.

'So Flynn wants my job? That's news to me. Flynn ain't got enough pull.'

Almost on top of his words came lively greetings in the bar in which the name of Dan Flynn was treated reverently.

'Get that greeting, Gus,' said Lil. 'That's Flynn now. Gettin' popular even in your own place. How d'you like that? Leave him to me, Gus; I'll work him in my own way.'

Flynn burst though the swinging doors, shaved, pomaded, and as meticulously groomed as ever, his hat cocked at a swagger angle.

'Hello, Gus,' he boomed in a voice that ricocheted about the walls of the dance-hall.

'Hello, Flynn,' Jordan said brusquely, and passed him, into the bar.

'Why did you send for me, Lil?' Flynn inquired giving her a flannel-mouthed grin.

'I'm always glad to see you, Flynn,' she rejoined. 'This time more than ever. Sit down. I got to thinkin' that maybe some day you may be boss of this here district, and maybe — '

Flynn adjusted his cigar and hooked a thumb in the usual armhole.

'Maybe then you might appreciate me?' He leaned close to her.

Lil gave him that flattering look.

'Something like that. You see, you're younger than Gus.'

The smile fled from Flynn's face and he seized her hand. 'You mean that, Lil?'

'Of course I mean it.'

'I've got as much right to have big aspirations as Jordan or any other man.'

"Course you have,' Lil told him, rewarding him with another devastating smile.

Flynn, still holding her hand, drew her closer.

'Say, Lil. Where do you think that Jordan gets all the coin to buy the powers that be; to make himself boss of this here district? To buy you them rocks? From this here place? Don't be a fool. It's them girls he ships down to Rio. The men down there like white women, and Jordan ships them down like cattle. He sells them outright as so much a head.'

'No! I can't believe it, Flynn!' Lil cried in mock horror.

'Well, it's true,' he assured her seriously, her mockery being wasted on him.

'And this guy "The Hawk" – is that why he's trailin' this here place? You don't know this here Hawk, do you, Flynn?'

Flynn's eyes sought the lower button of his waistcoat. '"The Hawk" is a big guy in the department. Ain't nobody that knows him. Even the men at headquarters wouldn't know him if they fell over him.' His tone changed to one of complete self-assurance. 'I ain't interested in this here Hawk. He ain't got nothin' on me.'

'What's he got on Jordan?' Lil pursued.

'White slave business ain't good business, Lil!'

'Flynn, you're pretty smart,' said Lil. 'I ain't never appreciated you before.' Her lips were near his, but as he leaned forward to kiss them they moved tantalizingly away.

She looked at him provocatively under her lashes.

'Look in tonight, Flynn,' she said in a tone that hinted more than it said. 'I might have something to say to you.'

'Lil!' Flynn cried in a hoarse whisper. Perspiration stood out on his brow. He moistened his lips. 'Lil! I'll be in tonight without fail. I – I've always wanted you!'

'Tonight,' said Lil, 'anything might happen. . . '

19

THE LAST WORD

LIL was worried far more than she was willing to admit even to herself. That Flynn had some damaging knowledge concerning Gus she was sure. She was certain, as well, that he was contemplating some course of action. It was not that she had anything really definite on which to pin that belief, yet she felt it instinctively, as one sometimes senses the approach of a thunderstorm long before the thunder is ever heard.

She wondered if it were possible for anything actually to happen to Gus. He was strong politically, wasn't he? But was he really big enough, if it came to a show-down, to fix things with the law, providing they had the goods on him?

What if all the power he thought he had, and which to a certain extent so far he had been able to wield, was suddenly shown to be shallow and ineffective? 'That'd be a hell of a note,' Lil told herself. If anything happened to Gus it would mean that she'd have to move on to other pastures. Not that she couldn't find them, and perhaps even greener ones. But she had had it pretty sweet here at Gus's. Now that she had Gus well house-broken, an innate laziness made her hate the prospect of starting all over again with somebody else in an unfamiliar bedroom.

She knew that even if Gus had to fade out of the picture

there would always be a man to take his place sooner or later. She had a few thousand stuck away and she had a half million in rocks hanging on her, hadn't she? Gus had said so. Well, she'd never again have to resort to peddling her stuff at so much a round.

There was Chick Clark. He wanted her to take up with him again. But he was like ancient history. After you read a couple of chapters of him you felt like turning to something lighter and more cheerful. No; she might have told Chick that she'd think about going back to him, but there wasn't any sense to that at all. Going back to him wasn't getting ahead none. And when you ain't getting ahead you're slipping, and you might as well begin thinkin' about where they'll bury you. Chick was not an asset. He was a liability. Liable to be jerked off his feet on the end of a rope for that little job of croakin' the gaol-screw.

She'd thought there for a while that something could be done with that Captain Cummings. She thought that she could educate the guy. But after that kiss he gave her she figured he'd probably go through life without ever unbuttonin' his pants, except when he was goin' to bed.

'He's the kind of guy that wants to be a brother to you,' she said to herself, at the remembrance of the kiss. And yet, Lil liked him better than my man she'd ever met, and one of the reasons was that he hadn't flung himself at her the way all the rest of them had. He had been aloof and self-contained; she had only sensed that she had broken down his guard when in her room he had called her Lillian. His voice had acquired at that moment a tender note. Lil didn't think of it as being 'tender'; to herself she named it as 'burning'.

She thought of him intensely. 'I don't know,' she argued with herself, 'it might be worth bein' holy for a while to land a guy like him. I guess he'd go for me all right if I was good. There ain't nothin' else the matter with me, God knows. I got everythin' a guy could want unless he was queer. I guess he thinks I ain't good enough for him. He figgers I'm low. Well, maybe I am, yet these here blue-bloods from uptown come down here and tell me I'm charmin'. What the hell! Life's a cock-eyed proposition no matter how you look at it.'

There was Flynn coming up tonight. She'd have to steam him up till his pulse got too fast for him, then he'd spill everything he had between his ears to her. She'd have to let him paw her around. That'd be all right if she liked him, but Flynn was in the same class with Rita. Sneaky, underhanded and double-crossing. Besides, he always smelled of tar soap, dead cigars and mange cure.

And there was 'The Hawk'. Who was he? If they only knew, maybe Gus could square him. If he had anything on Gus, how did he get it? It must've been through Flynn and Rita scheming together. And Rita – well, the eels had prob- ably eaten her lying tongue out by now. When Lil thought of Flynn and Rita, she hardened. She didn't love Gus, but he had been straight as a string with her, and she couldn't stand to see him done dirt, especially by birds like Flynn and Rita, who were supposed to be friends of his. She was glad now she had finished Rita. She didn't trouble Lil one bit. It was for Gus's sake she was worried.

While Lil was occupied with these far from pleasant thoughts, Gus came into her room. He too had a worried look, and Lil, noticing it, soon found out the reason for it.

He was the first to speak.

'It's damn' funny, Lil,' he said, 'that Rita ain't been in yet. It's got me worried.'

'Why?' demanded Lil. 'The evening's young yet.'

'I know,' Gus said, 'but she ain't nowhere to be found.'

Lil felt a quiver of alarm at that.

'What do you mean, Gus?' Lil inquired, busying herself with her nails. 'She ain't pulled her freight, has she?'

'I don't know what to think yet,' Gus went on. 'Charlie Fong ain't seen her, and at her hotel, the Cosmopolis, where she's been stayin' right along, she ain't been seen since yesterday. Her stuff's still there, I been inquirin' round like, and as far as I can figure out, after what you told me about her gettin' sore last night because Juarez gave you a diamond pin, why, it looks like you was about the last one to see her.'

Lil's heart skipped a beat, but she went on polishing her nails.

'Well, she left here. That's all I know.'

'By the way,' said Gus, 'let's see the pin Juarez gave you.'

'I ain't got it,' Lil replied. 'Rita said it was her pin, and I gave it back to her. I only took it from him because I didn't want to hurt his feelings.'

Jordan grunted.

'Rita didn't say anythin' about where she was goin' when she left here, did she?'

'No,' said Lil. 'Maybe she didn't know where she was goin'.'

'Humph,' said Jordan irritably. 'I never seen anythin' like it. Well, I got to find her, and that damn' quick.'

'Why don't you try draggin' the river for her?' Lil asked nonchalantly.

Jordan glared.

'What do you mean by that?' he demanded.

'Well,' said Lil. 'She's just the kind of dame to do the Dutch act over a guy.'

'Nonsense, Lil,' Gus retorted. 'Rita's too old a hand for that kind of thing.'

Lil lighted her cigarette, and, turning in her chair before the dressing-table, calmly faced him.

'Listen, Gus. It might be kind of convenient if Rita was dead right now, wouldn't it?'

'What!' he exclaimed. 'Hell, no! What gave you that wild idea?'

'Not so wild, Gus. Not so wild. Flynn says white slavery ain't good business, Gus.'

Gus's forehead grew pale above his bushy eyebrows.

'Why? Damn him! What does he mean? What does he mean?'

'I found out last night that Rita's been fixin' to give you the cross, Gus. Her and Flynn. Rita kind of let it slip in the heat of the argument.'

'Is that straight?' Jordan cried, wiping his brow with a handkerchief.

'I'm tellin' it to you, ain't I?' Lil snapped. 'And I wouldn't be surprised if Flynn spilled it all to this here Hawk, whoever he is. Flynn says he don't know him. But he's nothin' but a flannel-mouthed liar. I'm seein' him tonight, and I'm goin' to get the whole works out of him.'

Jordan's face made a transition from white to an apoplectic purple.

'If that's true about Flynn and Rita,' he ground out. 'I'll finish the both of them.'

'You don't need to worry about Rita, Gus,' Lil said slowly.

His mouth fell open, an he stared.

'You mean – she's dead?'

'I never mentioned the word, Gus,' said Lil.

There was a long moment of silence, and then with a peculiar glitter in his eyes Gus came over to her and his arm went around her shoulder. His voice came almost in a whisper.

'My God, Lil! You did – *that* – for *me*?'

Lil crushed out her cigarette.

'I gotta dress, Gus,' she said, and started to rise. Gus clasped her in his arms for a minute and kissed her. She smiled briefly into his eyes.

'I never meant for you to know anythin' about this business, ever, Lil,' Gus said earnestly.

'About what business?'

Gus shook his head.

'There ain't no one in this whole world like you, Lil,' he said, and, turning, he went out of the room with a firm step.

177

Lil drew a deep breath. Somehow her former worry had been lifted from her shoulders. Her conscience felt extraordinarily clear. Perhaps, she thought, the preachers were right when they said that confession was good for the soul. The captain had told her she had a soul. Of course, she hadn't made any out-and-out confession. But Gus had understood. 'Gus is a good-natured slob,' she told herself. 'Think of him figgerin' I knocked off Rita to protect him! Well, let him go on thinkin' it, if it makes him happy. And the best part of it is, Gus don't ask no embarrassin' questions. That's one thing I like about him.'

When Lil descended to the dance-hall to do her turn it seemed to her that she received a bigger ovation than ever before. The place was packed. There was hardly room enough to move in between the tables. They must have put in a lot of extra ones, she thought.

She received encore after encore, and she wound up by doing 'Easy Rider', and knocking them off their seats with it. Flynn was already there, and he tried to applaud louder than anybody else.

'Look at the lousy bastard,' she thought; 'he's thinkin' he's half-way to bed with me already. I wouldn't lay up with that guy if he had a diamond belly.'

She went over to his table as soon as they would let her off the floor. He got up and held a chair for her.

'I see you're a man of your word, Flynn,' he said flashing him a smile as she sat down.

'Honest men always keep their word, Lil,' said Flynn, pulling his chair close beside her. 'What'll you have to drink?'

'Some champagne.'

'Huh?' said Flynn, his eyes widening. Lil would be an expensive woman to keep.

'Sure,' Lil returned. 'Just tell the waiter. Gus always keeps some on ice for me.'

Flynn spoke to the waiter and turned back to her with an openly admiring look.

'You got good taste, Lil,' he said.

'So they tell me,' Lil rejoined. 'By the way, Gus has been lookin' for Rita. She ain't been around here. Have you seen her?'

'Who – me?' protested Flynn, looking away. 'No. Why should I see her?'

'I heard you was pretty friendly with her.'

'You got me wrong, Lil. Why I only spoke to the dame three or four times.'

'That's funny,' said Lil. 'Rita told me you two was as thick as flies in Delancey Street.'

The waiter brought champagne.

'Have some?' Lil offered Flynn.

'Kind of a lady's drink, ain't it, Lil?'

'Who told you that?' Lil demanded. 'Why, all the swells drink it. You gotta get class if you're gonna be boss of this here district.'

'Whatever you say, Lil,' Flynn returned. 'You learn me things, will you, Lil?'

'Why, sure. Say, I've learned guys more things in one night than they ever got out of four years in college.'

Flynn laughed.

'Start learnin' me right away, Lil.' He gulped down the champagne and smacked his lips.

'Yeah. Well, first thing, you don't drink champagne like it was beer. You sip it.'

'Oh, you sip it, huh?' He stared at the glass with its golden bubbles. He shook his head. 'I'm afraid I ain't got the patience for that, Lil.'

'Then you'll never be boss of this here district,' said Lil with mock severity. 'Anyhow, I don't see how you figger to get this thing away from Gus.'

Flynn frowned portentously.

'There's ways, Lil.'

'Of course,' she said. 'But what ways? Gus is pretty healthy. Don't look like he'll kick off for a while yet.'

Flynn haw-hawed.

'And I ain't waitin' that long either, Lil.'

'Well, now, look here,' said Lil, laying her hand over his and lowering her voice. 'If you an' me is goin' to get together, you gotta have a little confidence in me. I always start out with a clean sheet, Flynn.'

'You can count on a square deal from me, Lil,' Flynn declared earnestly.

'All right,' Lil said. 'Then lay your cards on the table and I'll tell your fortune.'

Lil's eyes, wandering for a moment beyond Flynn's shoulder, caught sight of Spider Kane picking his way with all possible speed among the closely jammed tables. There could be no mistake that he was heading her way. And there was something about him that gave her the impression of breathlessness. A shadowy crease came between her brows for an instant. What was up?

Flynn followed her glance, and throwing a look back over his shoulder also noticed Kane straining to reach them. But he turned back to the table with an annoyed grimace.

'As I was sayin', Lil . . . ' he began, when Kane arrived.

'Hello, Kane,' said Lil. 'You look winded. What's the matter?'

'I want to speak to you a minute, Lil,' he said, with a side glance at Flynn. 'It's private.'

'Oh, that's all right, Kane,' Lil told him. 'Flynn can hear.'

'Yeah, sure,' assented Kane. 'Chick Clark's out in the alley and he says he's gotta see you right away.'

'Hum,' said Lil to herself, 'this is gonna be pretty.'

'Chick Clark!' exclaimed Flynn with a dark look.

'Yeah,' replied Kane dryly. And to Lil: 'What'll I tell him?'

Lil barely hesitated, but in that instant her eyes swept the dance-hall and made note that Gus was not in evidence.

'Bring him up the back stairs to my room,' Lil instructed Kane.

'Don't be a fool, Lil!' cried Flynn. He'll kill you!'

There was something in that, too. Lil's eyes narrowed. A very definite idea clicked in her mind. Her heart beat rapidly. 'Two birds with one stone!' it beat. 'Two birds with one stone!'

'I ain't afraid of him, Flynn,' she said slowly and carefully. 'I'm dependin' on you to protect me. If you're goin' to be my man, now is the time to prove it.'

Kane turned quickly and went out through the bar.

Flynn stared at her for a moment and moistened his lips. Lil filled his glass with champagne. He drank it down thirstily. Then his hands sought his hip-pocket and caressed the butt of a pistol for an instant. He saw Lil's eyes upon him. He pressed her hand, and rose from the table, worked his way through the crowd of dancers and mounted the stairs leading from the dance floor to her room.

Lil watched him, oddly fascinated. She knew she had primed a dynamite charge by sending Chick to her room, and then applied the match by delegating Flynn to defend her against Clark's murderous intentions. She knew that death was all she could expect at the hands of Chick now, because she had failed to meet him at Kelly's when she had given her oath that she would do so. She had handled him neatly once. But she knew intuitively that there would be no stopping him this time.

Ragtime Kelly was pounding out a tango, but she wasn't even conscious of music until Juarez appeared suddenly as from nowhere and begged her to dance with him.

'I've waited so long all the night for this moment,' said Juarez with a smile.

Lil said nothing. Her eyes were upon Flynn, who was now

on the balcony before the door of her room, and looking down at her. She allowed herself to be drawn in Juarez's arms out on the dance floor and into the sweeping rhythm of the tango.

As Juarez swung her about, and as she felt his lips upon her shoulder, she saw Flynn open the door of her room.

Then came two spurts of flame and two shots resounded above the music like discordant counterpoint. Women screamed. The music stopped abruptly. Then Lil saw Flynn slowly crumple in the doorway. Over his fallen body sprang Chick Clark and down the stairs, the gun still smoking in his hand.

'Stick up your hands everybody!' he shouted. 'Don't move, any of you! I'll plug the first bird that bats an eye!'

All hands reached towards the ceiling. Clark backed towards the side door to the street, and then, turning quickly, dashed out.

Almost immediately came the sound of a police gong, and shrill blasts of police whistles. Then hell broke loose. Amidst the shrieks of the women patrons and the wild shouts of men, the overturning of tables and chairs as they made a mad rush for every available exit, came a swarm of the blue-coated officers of the law.

Lil remained rooted to the spot in the centre of the floor where she had ceased dancing. Juarez had vanished from her side. She was alone.

What was it all about? Was it Clark they were after? Why the raid? Was it Gus? Was this the end? The question pounded through Lil's consciousness. She felt no immediate fear for herself, but as yet nothing was clear. Things were happening too rapidly.

Then she saw Gus burst in from the bar-room as though the devil were at his heels. Two stalwart policemen seized him in a firm grasp. So it was Gus they were after! Well, he'd get out of it. They couldn't pin anything on him. Wasn't Rita dead? Oh, Rita! What did the cops know about her? Lil felt a sudden pang of fear. Her mind quickly brushed it aside. How could they know? And Flynn, with his big aspirations, was a stiff. There isn't a good squawk in a million dead! They couldn't hang nothin' on her.

'Put Jordan in the wagon, Sergeant,' a voice rang out behind her in tones that were harsh and commanding. It cut through to her marrow. Yet, why should it have a familiar echo? She turned her head to the speaker.

It was Captain Cummings. But a different Captain Cummings. His handsome face was hard and his eyes orbs of steel.

Lil gave a faint gasp. This was a blow below the belt, and she hadn't been prepared to take it. What was he doing here? Why was he ordering those coppers around? What in hell did the Salvation Army have to do with raiding a joint?

Lil saw the familiar figure of Officer Doheny coming towards her and the look on his face was not pleasant to see. Doheny was gloating over the opportunity to settle old scores. Lil knew how he felt. She could have spat in his eye.

Captain Cummings turned to Doheny.

'Never mind. I'll take care of her,' he barked.

Crestfallen, Doheny faded out of the picture, Lil's sneer following him like a bloodhound.

'What the hell is this?' roared Jordan, struggling in the arms of his captors. 'I'm the boss of this here district and I'll tell you — '

Captain Cummings wheeled upon him.

'You'll tell the jury what you know about the white slave traffic.'

'Damn you!' Jordan snarled.

'We've got the goods on you, Jordan,' the captain said sharply.

'So that's it!' Lil exclaimed to herself. That sin-chaser mucking around with the bulls. Gum-shoeing himself into the confidence of people while they trusted him because of his calling.

'So you're "The Hawk"!' sneered Jordan.

'That's what they call me,' Cummings snapped. The mask was off now. No use denying it.

'"The Hawk"!' cried Lil, a sinking feeling mingling with a growing rage. '"The Hawk"! A night-bird workin' in the dark! Stealin' the confidence of people. The lowest kind of a thief—' Cummings faced her, a deep red crawling up from under his collar.

'Cut it, Lil,' warned Jordan. 'It's our finish.' He shot Cummings a contemptuous look. 'I always knew there was something phony about you!'

'Take him away,' commanded the captain.

Lil made a protesting step towards Gus, but Cummings stopped her.

'What are you going to do with her?' Jordan demanded.

'Never mind,' he said roughly, and added with a touch of sarcasm: 'She'll be well taken care of.'

Jordan fought to get free of the restraining hands.

'You stool-pigeon! You rat! You can't get away with this!'

They forced him out into the street. Lil began to wonder why she had ever had a thought that life could grow monotonous. Gus was gone, and if she ever saw him again it would probably be through bars that had nothing to do with dispensing of liquors. She grew suddenly cold with hatred as she turned to the man who had posed as an agent of God, while he had been nothing but an agent of the Law of man.

'"The Hawk"!' said Lil, throwing into the word all the venom of contempt that she could bring to it.

'As an officer of the law,' he said coldly, 'I'm only doing my duty.'

'Your duty,' she sneered. 'First it was your duty to bring me to God. Tonight it's your duty to take me to gaol.'

He took a step towards her, but before Lil could learn the intention of his move, Juarez, who had been hiding under the bar, came through the shattered doors, which sagged on twisted hinges. He ran to her with arms outstretched.

'Ah, you are in trouble, Babee!' he cried. 'Come, fly weeth me to Rio. I love you more than anytheeng in the world. My Babee – my Babee!'

Lil rolled her eyes heavenward. If she went into a convent to take the veil, she thought, she'd find that guy Juarez under her bed.

'What the hell!' shouted Cummings in disgust, and seizing the passionate Juarez by the scruff of his neck and slack of his trousers flung him out into the bar. 'Get out of here! Get out of here, before you get hurt!'

Juarez, with inflammable Latin curses on his lips, broke for the street.

'Take care of Babee!' Cummings murmured as he returned to where Lil stood defiantly.

She was beautiful in her anger, he told himself. She was flame! A man wouldn't be a man if he didn't long to snuff that flame! How many men had tried to? And how many had been consumed in the attempt? He was wrong when he told her that diamonds had no warmth, that they seemed cold to him. Why, her diamonds were tiny meteors that shed sparks across the heaven of her voluptuousness!

He strode towards her, but before he could reach her he was interrupted by the entrance of Chick Clark, who, hand-cuffed to two police officers, was literally foaming at the mouth with rage. If his eyes had been torches they would have burned Lil to ashes.

'You tipped off the bulls I was at Kelly's!' he screamed at her. 'You was the only one knew I was there. When I got away and came over here you sent that rat upstairs to get me. But I got him first. If I had a gat I'd blow your brains out!' With a violent, almost superhuman show of strength he almost reached her, dragging the officers with him. Cummings stepped in front of Lil, and the two policemen regained control of Chick.

'This time they got me for murder,' he shouted, 'but if ever I get out of this I'll kill you! I'll get you! To hell with you, blast you! I'll get you! You can't double-cross me!'

They dragged Chick away amid a flood of threats and curses. 'You can finish that on the end of a rope,' Lil murmured.

Again Lil and the false soul-saver were alone. All Lil's anger had melted away. Her mind was beginning to function again; to run in normal channels. Her wits were starting to take hold of things and adjust themselves to the new order. This time, when she spoke, her voice took on a new tone. A hurt tone, strangely appealing. Lil had by no means exhausted her bag of tricks.

'You makin' me think I was a lost soul or something,' she flung at him. 'Me layin' off my diamonds one by one. Layin' off my paint and powder. Layin' awake nights thinkin' I wasn't good enough for you. And you – just a common ordinary cop.' She paused with just the right amount of dramatic effectiveness. 'All right, Mr. Policeman, do your business. Go ahead and give me the bracelets. It'll be a new kind of jewellery for me.' She extended her wrists to him. He made no move towards her now. But there was a strange light in his eyes.

'Well, what are you waiting for?' Lil asked. 'Let me tell you, I'll go down in history with some mighty fine people. John the Baptist did a little time, you know. I told you I read your Bible.' She paused. He still regarded her with a peculiar expression. Again she extended her arms to him.

'Well, what are you standing there for?' she demanded. 'What are you waiting for? You want me, don't you?'

And then he did what Lil wanted him to do; had hoped for, but hardly dared expect. He seized her wrists but drew her fiercely to him.

'You *know* I want you!' he cried in a voice tense with feeling.

Lil continued to play the game. 'Let me go!'

'I'm never going to let you go,' he said, holding her still tighter and his lips caressing the hair by her ear.

'You know what I am, don't you?' Lil protested with calculating weakness.

Cummings rose to the bait.

'I know better than you think I do,' he assured her softly. 'I know that giving Jacobsens's Hall to the Salvation Army isn't the only good thing you've done.'

'I did it for you,' Lil admitted with charming simplicity.

His lips were almost on hers when he said:

'Then you'll believe me when I tell you that I'm mad about you. I want you!'

A wild gladness surged up within her at the words which told her that the man she had wanted for so long was hers; yet, she asked herself: 'Is this love? Really love? Or something just for the winter season?'

But her self-confidence had returned to her completely, and it was sweet triumph. As her lips were crushed hotly to his she murmured:

'I always *knew* you could be *had*!'

Other Virago Books of Interest

THE CONSTANT SINNER

MAE WEST

Introduction by Kathy Lette

Babes Gordon, a broad who 'would not have known what a moral was if it could be made to dance naked in front of her', is the audacious heroine of this spirited lowlife novel set in Thirties Harlem. Seducing and discarding lovers according to her whim (or her eye for the main chance) Babes ensnares first an innocent young boxer, then a handsome chainstore heir, blithely ignoring mobster Money Johnson, due to leave jail soon. Surrounded by characters like Cokey Jenny, Liverlips Sam, Pinhead Pete and the Black Tulips, Babes shamelessly schemes her way through outrageous shenanigans. Glorious and delicious . . . Mae West, the Hollywood legend, continues to entertain.